THE
PELICAN

ALSO BY MARTIN MICHAEL DRIESSEN

Rivers

THE
PELICAN

A Comedy

MARTIN
MICHAEL
DRIESSEN

TRANSLATED BY JONATHAN REEDER

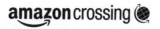
amazoncrossing

Text copyright © 2017 by Martin Michael Driessen
Translation copyright © 2019 by Jonathan Reeder

Previously published as *De Pelikaan* by Uitgeverij Van Oorschot in the Netherlands in 2017. Translated from Dutch by Jonathan Reeder. First published in English by Amazon Crossing in 2019.

Published by Amazon Crossing, Seattle

www.apub.com

ISBN-13: 9781542044875 (hardcover)
ISBN-10: 1542044871 (hardcover)
ISBN-13: 9781542044868 (paperback)
ISBN-10: 1542044863 (paperback)

Cover design by Joan Wong

Printed in the United States of America

First edition

He who dies, dies as he was.

—Antoine de Saint-Exupéry, *Flight to Arras*

PART 1

The town on the Adriatic coast had once been part of the Ottoman and then the Habsburg Empire, and now belonged to Yugoslavia. Nothing much ever changed; indeed, if the postman Andrej had made his rounds a hundred years earlier, he would have done so in essentially the same town as now. Dilapidated houses had been replaced by others in a similar architectural style; only higher up the gray hills did one find modern housing tracts with concrete apartment buildings, but these were not on Andrej's route, namely the old district, the labyrinth of alleys and lanes above the harbor boulevard, whose only appeal, in the sense of urban design, lay in the People's Square and the former archducal residence.

The boulevard had been beautified with a long row of palm trees, planted long ago for an official visit by Tito. Seeing as there was little tourism to speak of, the parking ban was in fact entirely superfluous and consequently had been ignored for years.

The fishing harbor was picturesque, as was the azure coastline both to the north and to the south; there was a funicular railway, and the town could boast of a clock museum second to none. Yet despite these distinctive qualities, it was a wallflower of European history. Nothing happened here; the town had brought forth and buried one generation after another without a single one of its citizens leaving a mark on the world.

Perhaps the apparent attractions were in fact its fatal flaws: it was pretty, but too small and not attractive enough to compete with cities like Zadar and Dubrovnik. Praised in Baedekers for a hundred years, the town still never caught on as a tourist destination. And it had no industry, hardly any commerce, and the coastal region was, agriculturally speaking, of little consequence.

Aside from the clock museum, it was mostly the pelicans that lent the town its allure. Pink pelicans, which returned every year and occupied the boulevard—these improbable creatures, well-nigh messianic in appearance, fed off the town for a few months before returning to Africa.

The houses were high ceilinged, and the tall windows had heavy wooden shutters, the slats narrowly cracked open with a hook during the cool morning and evening hours. The stairwells were all narrow and airless. There was no sense of going to or coming from somewhere; one simply preferred to stay put. The electrical wiring was prehistoric; it was not only poorly insulated but haphazardly installed, and dated from so long ago that the townspeople regarded it as a sort of atavistic system of roots and thought it best to leave well enough alone. The same went for the water supply and the sewer system.

Additionally, the town had a hard-to-reach dog racetrack, located on a dusty field to the east of the salt ponds.

The funicular railway had been installed in 1892 by the same civil engineer who had built the famous Nerobergbahn in Wiesbaden. It was a technical wonder that conquered the difference in elevation between the lower station and the Orthodox church at the top of the hill entirely without motorized assistance, thanks to the patented principle of water ballast in the descending car, whose counterweight pulled a second car uphill. The ballast level was maintained with water drawn from a reservoir farther up in the mountains, so that the funicular operated at practically no cost. Although it was once popular as a tourist attraction, nowadays virtually no one visited the monument to the heroes of socialism that now stood at the spot once occupied by the church, destroyed in the war. Only Josip Tudjman, the funicular's machinist and conductor, spent his lunch break there every afternoon.

Normally he operated the funicular on his own, which meant taking the steep path from the lower station up to the car parked above in order to fill it with water ballast, and then returning down to man the booth. The original operating regulations required a machinist to be on each car, but these days, the passengerless car could travel unmanned.

Josip lived a stone's throw from the lower station and could just as well go home for his midday meal, but he was unhappily married, and preferred to close the booth for an hour and take one of the mahogany cars up to the monument to spend that time on his own.

In fact, Josip was a real-life example of the larger-than-life, rousing bronze heroes of the fatherland who, bayonets thrust forward, appeared poised to charge off the pedestal on which he unpacked his lunch box; for he was a war veteran, decorated with the Order of the People's Army, which was also the reason he had been given this job.

As he sat atop the gray hill, chewing his salami and gazing out over the unrippled sea and the town at his feet and the straight double tracks of his funicular, his head was clear. This was Josip's preferred state of mind, because, he knew, contemplation only led to worry: about his child, and about how the woman who was its mother could further torment him. If nothing happened, then at least nothing bad happened. He removed his cap and leaned against the bronze boot of a socialist hero.

At precisely two o'clock, he filled the reservoir of the waiting car, set it in motion, and made his way downhill to reopen the booth. Sometimes he descended on foot, to save himself another trip back up. In addition to running the funicular, he was licensed to sell state lottery tickets, and in front of the kiosk was a metal magazine carousel, which did not bring in much, but nor did it cost him anything. The only one who purchased anything except the local newspaper was the postman Andrej; he would not only buy a lotto ticket every week but would take anything with a color photo, preferably one of Princess Diana.

In his younger years, Andrej had been a first-string player on the local soccer team, initially as a striker and, later, as goalkeeper. He was very tall; this, however, did not give him much of an advantage as a goalkeeper, as he was clumsy and basically unathletic. He had always regarded his above-average height as something special until it became clear to him that this, along with his extremely large nose and his oversized feet, tended to be the subject of ridicule. He never forgave mankind for that.

Every day he needed about five hours to sort and deliver the mail. He preferred to make his rounds at midday rather than in the morning coolness, for nearly everyone slept in the afternoon behind the closed shutters, and aside from a few cats he had the town to himself. His bicycle had a high frame, a double crossbar, a crate for packages above the front wheel, and two rubberized saddlebags, one on either side of the rear fork. Andrej saw himself as the link between the town and the outside world. He pushed his heavy bicycle, its bags usually nearly empty, through the steepest alleys, carried it up stairs where necessary, and at the end of his route he coasted along the paved Nikole Zrinskog back down to the harbor, where he lived. Only then would he remove his black cap and lock the bike, which after all was the property of the postal service, to the bars in front of the window of his semi-basement apartment.

He had started opening people's mail early in his career. He liked to imagine that Marshal Tito would have decorated him for his vigilance, and for thwarting potential capitalist plots.

He steamed open the envelopes in his kitchenette, and after having inspected the contents on the Formica tabletop, he carefully glued them back shut. Even though he never discovered anything significant, the skillful application of his pursuit gave him great satisfaction. But Tito was dead, and Princess Grace of Monaco, too, and since then the world had not been the same.

Andrej went to the beach in search of a new woman in his life. It was a promisingly blue September day, and she would have to be a foreigner, because he invariably struck out with the local women and girls. He wore swimming trunks and a short-sleeved shirt unbuttoned halfway. He put on sunglasses he had found long ago on a bench on the boulevard, but they were so dark and scratched that he hardly saw anything through them. For a brief moment he thought his dream just might become reality. On the boulders at the waterline in front of the Hotel Esplanade, a young woman in a bikini lay sunning herself, alone. She lay on her back, one white leg bent at the knee.

Andrej approached cautiously, if only because he saw nearly nothing through the sunglasses. He bent over every now and then, pretending to gather seashells.

If she had noticed him, she did not let on. Her legs were spread wide apart on the beach towel, so that from close by and without the sunglasses, he could see the curve of her vulva under the fabric of her bikini bottom. He couldn't tell yet if she was pretty, or whether they might have a future together, but it was worth a try.

"Hello," he said. "I'm Andrej."

She did not reply. Next to her on the beach towel sat a hotel key on an enormous brass ball, and a bottle of Piz Buin suntan lotion.

"Can I offer you an ice cream? Esplanade has really good sorbets."

If she was an American, as he hoped, she wouldn't understand him, of course. But she answered in Croatian: "Great. Lemon."

When he returned she sat up and he saw that she did indeed have breasts, which he had doubted at first when he saw her lying flat on her back; they were quite small, and they appeared to be rather far apart, just like her eyes. She ate the ice cream and glanced at him now and then. It was unbelievably intimate.

"I could go for another one," she said.

"Me, too!" Andrej said, nearly shouting, and he raced up the wooden steps to the Esplanade's ice cream stand.

They appeared to be kindred spirits. Within half an hour he had told her everything about himself, and she said that her favorite color was purple.

"What incredible luck that we've met," he said. "If I'd been on duty, then we would have missed each other."

"What kind of work do you do?" she asked.

"I'll tell you in a sec," he answered, his smile carrying a whiff of mystery, and he got up, as agile as a camel.

When he returned with yet another round of sorbets, she was sitting in the sand, and cigarette smoke hovered above her head. This put him off; he disapproved of women smoking, certainly outside the home. They would have to have a word about this. But what ensued was even worse. A squid had washed ashore; she held it between her thighs and was busy tying its tentacles into knots.

"You can't do that!" he shouted, horrified.

"Oh no?" she replied, the filter cigarette clenched between her teeth. "Why not? Just look at this stupid, ugly creature." She tugged at the ends of the helplessly wriggling tentacles.

"Leave him be!"

"What, can't you take it?" she mocked, and her cigarette hissed as she stubbed it out on the squid's body.

"You're cruel!"

"And you're a loser," she laughed back.

As he turned, he could hear the splash of the creature being tossed back into the sea.

He was out of sorts for three weeks after that incident. There was no goddess like Princess Grace anymore. Diana was good-looking, but not really regal enough, and Sophia Loren was not his type.

If the world was such a callous place, he pondered as he put on the kettle, you might as well go with the flow. He had taken an envelope from today's mail and steamed it open. This one was interesting, because it was addressed to a box number.

A letter addressed to a newspaper box number was almost always in response to a personal ad: man seeking woman or woman seeking man. This was simply human nature.

He recognized the handwriting on the envelope at once. If you want to stay anonymous, he thought, then at least take the trouble of writing in block letters. What a loser, that Josip Tudjman. He saw this handwriting every week on the receipts for the magazines he delivered to the kiosk. What was Josip Tudjman up to? he wondered.

It was a letter to a lady in Zagreb, who had sought contact with "a kindly, charming gentleman, age not important." He suggested planning their first rendezvous at his funicular, or, if she preferred, at a café in Zagreb. The letter was formal but clumsy; he, Andrej, would have formulated it more elegantly. Tudjman did not give his address, which was entirely understandable, considering his wife's pathological jealousy, but had offered the telephone number of the funicular station, which was rather clever of him.

Andrej decided to photograph the letter. He laid it in the stripe of sunlight that shone through the bars of his semi-basement window onto the Formica tabletop, and got out his Kodak. He set the f-stop to a small aperture, as he had done for the photos of the butterflies on the cherry blossoms, which had been used as postcard motifs. He used a tripod to facilitate a long shutter time. He had no enlarger himself, although his apartment was in fact the ideal place for a darkroom. And he couldn't have this roll of film developed in town, for old Schmitz, who had also printed his butterfly pictures, inspected every negative meticulously. He would have to get the film processed elsewhere.

The opportunity presented itself when his former soccer club went to Rijeka for an away game, and he could travel with them on the team bus. Before halftime he left the stadium and walked into town; eventually his eye fell upon a small photography shop on the boulevard, near a hotel. They probably developed tourist snapshots there every day, he thought, and would not pay much attention to the pictures themselves. The prints would be ready the next day, which meant either not returning home on the team bus or making another trip to Rijeka. It was too risky, of course, to leave an address with the photo shop. He got back to the field in time to see his team lose 8–0 and made a drastic decision: he would stay in Rijeka overnight. He told the coach, who was heaving sports bags into the hold of the bus as though they were cadavers in body bags, that he wanted to stay and see the city's sights.

"Suit yourself," he said.

And so it happened that Andrej stayed overnight in a hotel for the first time in his life. Everything about it was off-putting; even the musty-smelling bed did nothing to reassure him. A continuous stream of cars drove past, and the flimsy curtains in his room did little to block out the light. But it was worth the trouble, for at eleven o'clock the next morning he paid eight dinars and was given a slender manila envelope with his photos, the negatives tucked into a separate, narrower pocket.

The five photos of Tudjman's letter were practically identical. They could be deciphered with a magnifying glass, although after all, Tudjman knew full well what he had written.

Andrej was exhilarated. He was privy to a secret known to no one else. As he pushed his bicycle up the steep alleyways and caught sight of the funicular rising above the town's rooftops toward the crest of the hill with the monument to the heroes, he thought, I could bring those cars to a standstill if I wanted.

Not that he had any personal grudge against Tudjman. He hardly knew him; they didn't even go to the same café. Of course, he knew that Tudjman was a decorated veteran, and for that reason he almost regretted him being the victim. But fate, Andrej knew, was impartial; even Marshal Tito himself had sacrificed former comrades and friends in the name of the cause.

Josip's wife was a horror. The signs of instability she had already exhibited early on should have been a warning sign; however, she was a young lass with an ample bosom and a friendly, round baby face, so there was no reason a certain lack of intelligence should have put him off. Besides, having experienced the horrors of war, he yearned only for a straightforward, safe existence. The fact that their first child, Mirko, lived only six months did not discourage him. But then Katarina was born with a cleft lip and only started to learn to speak at the age of six; she was a crazed and slow-witted child, although at times she and Josip managed to achieve something like closeness, as when she had taken her medicine and they set to work on a large jigsaw puzzle—always the same one—picturing a white mare and a white foal in a field of dandelions. This child, he could have lived with. But his wife had been transformed into something unforeseen, something unfathomable. She cursed, she ranted, she groused incessantly, and was consumed by compulsive jealousy. They could no longer walk down the street together without her attacking him for greeting a female neighbor; on the other hand, if he did not greet her and shuffled past with downcast eyes, his wife hissed at him that it was as plain as day that he had to force himself not to ogle her. The funicular, she claimed, was a playground for shameless foreign sluts who would spread their legs for a free ride. The fatter and more formless she became, the more she seemed to revel in her own ugliness. Her face had become rounder, and as dark and wrinkled as a walnut, and the fact that her light-blue eyes, amid all this repulsiveness, remained the same as those of the young girl he once courted only made things worse. For a long time, the neighbors did their best, but in the end were forced to concede that Josip was doomed to a life of misery.

The first letter he wrote since the death of his mother was to a lady in Zagreb in response to a personal advertisement.

She was a still-young woman who, according to her ad, sought a "kindly, charming gentleman," age not important, as long as he was cultivated.

Josip then had sex for the first time in years, and after that he took the bus to Zagreb once every six weeks.

What especially excited him was that she always wore spike heels and showed a lively interest in the history of funicular techniques.

The day had arrived. Andrej observed how Tudjman—clearly recognizable, for he was the only passenger in the car—rode up the hill to enjoy his midday break in the shade of the monument. When the funicular came to a stop and the cars had reached their starting and ending positions, he mounted his bicycle and rode slowly down the Ulica Nikole Tesle, a broad paved road lined with plane trees, on which the funicular's lower station was located.

He had snipped out letters and words for his blackmail note, like he had seen on that TV show *Columbo*. This turned out to be a time-consuming task, all the more because he had to carefully cut around the photos of Princess Diana. And now he had extremely persuasive evidence in his possession, far better than Tudjman's correspondence.

Three weeks earlier, while making his deliveries at the plaza where the bus stops were located, he saw Josip Tudjman, in his green uniform, as always, waiting with a bunch of flowers in his hand. This was suspicious. Andrej feigned not to have seen him and cycled hastily on.

He did not bother to eat, leaving the plate of anchovies untouched on the kitchen table; he changed out of his postman's uniform into short pants, a polo shirt, sandals, and a straw hat, and grabbed his camera bag. He filled an empty Sinalco bottle with tap water, for it was a hot day and the ride was a long one.

Aside from the funicular and the steep, zigzagging footpath alongside it, the only way to reach the heroes' monument was by road, first heading southward along the coast, and then taking the first side road up into the mountains, until a white arrow-shaped sign pointed to the turnoff leading to the reservoir. It was an uninviting route, and few people saw any reason to visit a fishless and sterile dammed lake high in the limestone hills.

It had thus been a good ten years since Andrej was last there. He chained his bicycle to a concrete picnic bench, hung his camera bag around his neck, and set out parallel to the shore path to his right, the shortest route to the monument and the upper station of the funicular railway. If his suspicions were correct, then Tudjman and the lady from Zagreb would now be making out on the pedestal of the monument.

In the event that they were cautious enough to have chosen the back side of the monument, then he would pretend to be photographing insects in the reeds. But he considered this unlikely. Anyone in a romantic state of mind would certainly prefer a view of the bay and the sea rather than the barren hinterland. And Tudjman, the pathetic braggart, would want to impress her, and would therefore use the funicular, which, Andrej mused, should still have been government property. Tudjman would want to spread the magnificent panorama of the town and coastline at her feet, as though he had personally conquered the place himself, while in fact he should thank his lucky stars the new owners hadn't fired him.

Andrej crept up the steps to the monument on all fours until he reached the platform, his camera at the ready. If they caught him, he would say he was taking artistic photographs of the vista, with the bronze boots and the trampled fascist insignias in the foreground. The Kodak was both his weapon and his alibi.

His precautions were unnecessary. Tudjman and his lady friend, who wore a flowered dress and a white hat, were entirely engrossed in one another, entwined in a compromising embrace on the bottom step. Next to them were two glasses and a bottle of spumante.

Andrej began snapping pictures. His heart stood still with every click of the shutter, but they apparently did not hear or see him, even though the woman's face—or what he could see of it above Tudjman's shoulder—was turned toward him for quite some time.

He dared not load a new roll of film, but the sixteen shots he took would suffice. Tudjman and the lady kissing, toasting, embracing. The lady rolling up her stockings. Tudjman's hand on her knee. The lady on his lap.

This was the moment. Andrej rested his bicycle on its kickstand and glanced around. No one in sight. And in any case, he was a uniformed postman, he could put an envelope in the kiosk's mailbox without raising any suspicions.

The cable car tracks and the monument were obscured by the foliage of the plane trees. There wasn't a soul to be seen, and he recognized all the parked cars.

He did not see anything particularly wrong with what he was doing. After all, Tudjman was a married man and a father, and had no business dallying with another woman. Perhaps the three-thousand-dinar payoff would serve as a kind of moral warning shot. He had originally planned to demand two thousand, but on second thought he felt that all the costs he had incurred justified an extra thousand. And besides, Tudjman could spare the money; in addition to his pension he had an income from the funicular.

Not that it was about the money. It was about the need for something to happen in Andrej's life; this total denial of his existence simply had to stop. The world owed him something. Once he thrust the letter through the chute of the green cast-iron mailbox, there would be no turning back. It would be the first time in his life that he took a step that was courageous and irreversible.

Never before had he sped down the Nikole Zrinskog at such a clip; he whipped along the ring road that led him around the alleys and nooks and crannies of the old town center to the harbor. The Agip gas station flew past, the ruins of the Turkish fort, the dusty palm trees, the long row of deserted terraced workmen's houses that followed the stepped contour of the hillside, like the spine of a dead animal. He coasted all the way, sitting upright on the seat, his legs stretched forward as though going down a playground slide, pant legs flapping, until he had to brake in the last curve before the boulevard. He set his bicycle against the bars and, as always, chained it securely. After all, the bicycle was state property, and with it came certain responsibilities.

Andrej wanted to watch Tudjman return to the kiosk after his lunch break, oblivious to what awaited him. Only he, Andrej, knew.

He bought an ice cream and headed for the jetty on the waterfront. It was a warm day for this time of year, sunny and practically windless. Only far off to the south, where it was cloudy, did the coastline become hazier.

He walked out to the end of the jetty and sat down on a low wall. One thirty. There was hardly a ripple on the water underneath him, where small fish darted back and forth, apparently taking no notice of the up-and-down swells that carried their entire school.

He tossed the last bite of his cone into the water and smiled at the pattern that emerged: lightning-quick attacks followed by brief retreats, as if every sinking crumb was a depth charge that first had to be deactivated. And then the school continued to swell back and forth like foolish children in an oversized cradle who had no inkling of the big wide world around them.

He looked at his watch, and then over his shoulder. The cable car was still stationary. A large pelican had approached, stopping about four meters away.

All his life, Andrej had seen the pelicans descend on the town each year. He had never liked them. They were odd creatures and did not belong here. Moreover, they were an unpleasant reminder of the time he was unemployed, before he had gotten his current job: he had earned extra cash by donating blood, and the blood bank's emblem was a pelican. It had something to do with the Christian faith.

"Go away," he shouted, waving his arms.

The pelican stood there and looked straight at him with its beady eyes. It had the kind of dignity one sometimes sees in very ugly and stupid creatures.

"Piss off to Africa," Andrej said, and got up. He gave the pelican a wide berth, for they were pretty big animals, and returned to the harbor.

The first envelope was postmarked Rijeka and contained photographs of Jana and him. Jana was the woman of his dreams, the woman who made him happier than he had been in years. Without the accompanying note, he would have treasured the pictures and even proudly shared them with her: they had been taken during that first, memorable rendezvous at his funicular. It was the first time Jana had visited him, after months of his traveling to Zagreb on the bus to be with her.

They were small-format prints with a jagged white border. On the back, the stamp of the photo studio where the film had been developed had been blacked out with thick ink strokes.

Together with the photos was a note demanding three thousand dinars. The note was a chaotic collage of glued-on letters and words that, Josip could tell at once, had been largely snipped out of the celebrity magazines *Paris Match* and *Bunte* and the local newspaper.

His first reaction was: What's three thousand dinars, after all? He could afford it. But then he thought: Why am I acting like this is a household bill or the monthly rent? This is about Jana, the love of my life, and no one has any business interfering with us. This is gross, unlawful blackmail. And what's more, he had watched enough television to know you should never give in to the demands of a blackmailer, because that's the beginning of the end.

OR ELSE YOUR FRAU WILL FIND OUT EVERYTHING read the last sentence, haphazardly pieced together out of letters of irregular fonts and sizes.

The word *Frau* had been snipped out of the *Bunte*.

An envelope containing the money, said the instructions, was to be placed under a certain concrete block along the Ulica Zrinskog by one thirty the following Tuesday afternoon. That was when, as everyone in the town knew, he took the cable car up the hill for his lunch break.

And the concrete block was on a barren, vacant stretch of the ring road, and could not be observed from the monument. There was only a small bus shelter, where no one could conceal themselves from a watchful eye. It seemed impossible, then, to catch whoever came to collect the money.

There's no getting out of this, he realized. But he did decide to write a letter back, making it perfectly clear that this one payoff was also, definitively, the last.

Andrej was elated. The three thousand dinars in the envelope meant more to him than his postman's salary. This was money he had earned through personal enterprise, money he would never have had without having shown such nerve and gumption. A socialist utopia was all well and good, and while he was in favor of equal opportunity and against international capitalism, over time it was a bit suffocating to realize that being better than the others, that being someone special, made no difference whatsoever. And he was not planning to spend the rest of his life as a nobody. A man like him deserved more. The waiting list for a modern apartment on the outskirts of town was so long that it would take a bachelor like him years to get one; that he, of all people, who literally towered head and shoulders above the others, had to squeeze himself into a semi-basement apartment was a grave injustice.

After all, on the soccer field, too, it was always the top players who walked off with the honors. And the Russian cosmonauts were heroes because, like Andrej, they were the first to venture into the unknown.

For a moment he considered stowing the banknotes in the drawer of his nightstand forever; this money was too meaningful to spend.

The accompanying letter likewise gave him immense satisfaction, and he reread it several times. Josip Tudjman gave notice that this would be the first and last payoff. But of course, the decision in this matter lay entirely with Andrej. Actually, Tudjman was begging him not to make further demands. The fact that he'd paid proved he was powerless.

In the end, Andrej decided to spend the money on something special. He cycled out to the dog racetrack on the edge of town.

When he arrived and, as always, chained his bicycle, this time to the rusty railing, a dust cloud rose at the far end of the oval track. He had missed half of the first race, but there would be more. Farther up, a cluster of cars parked haphazardly on the gray-green field surrounded the focal point of the event: a small group of men at a white party tent and a dilapidated shed. Folk music blared from loudspeakers. Andrej could see at once that he did not know these men. He had suspected as much when he saw their cars: rickety Zastavas, cast-offs from Italy, a few small trucks. The spectators doubtless came mainly from the concrete apartment blocks where he did not deliver the mail, and perhaps also from the countryside.

He was out of place here, but did not mind. He came as a man who could blow three thousand dinars if he felt like it. The dogs, with their muzzles and colorful vests, each emblazoned with a number on the back, tore around the racetrack at breakneck speed, passing him as he walked along the railing.

The metallic riff of a Slovenian pop group was broken off for the announcement that Darling Boy had won.

Money was paid out, betting tickets discarded, the heavily distorted voice from the loudspeaker announced that the next race would commence in fifteen minutes, and the music resumed.

Andrej bought an ice-cold can of cola and studied the racing form. Greyhounds at 240 meters. He didn't understand a jot of it, but no matter. He would bet high, that's what he was here for.

"You fellows have a tip for me?" he asked jovially of the bystanders, his wallet in his hand.

The men did not answer; he could see they were sizing him up, perhaps estimating how they might profit from this visit from an outsider. But Andrej felt self-assured.

"Win, forecast, or trio?" someone asked.

"Win," Andrej replied confidently, so as not to let on that he had no idea what they were talking about.

"Bet on Laika, then." The tipster was a small, unshaven man in a tweed jacket and jogging pants, with a chewed-off cigarillo in the corner of his mouth.

Laika, that was the name of the first living being in outer space.

"Why Laika?" Andrej asked, a bundle of banknotes in his hand.

"Fastest bitch last year," the man replied, with a knowing nod.

Andrej bet three hundred dinars on Laika.

By the time he cycled home he had lost more than a thousand dinars. But he had no regrets: he saw it as a useful lesson, and on top of it, one he had not had to pay for out of his own pocket. Laika, it turned out, was old and slow and finished last, and in the next race, Drago, the favorite, was beaten by Golden Dream. He resolved to return the following week and approach things more wisely: he would spread his bets, and would wager "reverse forecast," meaning he only had to choose the first- and second-place dogs, regardless of their order. This was less risky. And most of all, he would no longer listen to the small man with the tweed jacket who, he noticed after the fact, did not bet on Laika or Drago but, in both cases, on the winning dog.

On his next visit to the dog races he lost most of the blackmail money. A few times, though, he came close: his dogs finished first and third, then second and fourth; but he did not win. Not even once. Laika was in the starting box for the last race, although probably no one bet on her. As it happened, things went even worse for her than last time, because when the gates swung open, she did not leave her box at all. As the other greyhounds tore into the first curve, leaving a red dust cloud behind them like a quick-burning fuse, her owner, a stout Gypsyish man in a leather jacket, approached the starting gate and started hitting the bars and prodding her with a stick. Laika crept out of the box, to the great amusement of the spectators, her tail between her legs and her scrawny back hunched. She watched her rivals, now on the far side of the track, as they reached their top speed, let her narrow head droop, and lifted a front paw, as though to show an injury. The announcer provided witty commentary throughout, and as the tractor towed away the starting boxes to clear the track for the finish, her owner clipped on her leash and led her to the small shed that served as a kennel.

Andrej bought another ice-cold cola and ambled among the cars parked randomly on the open field, in order to be alone and gather his thoughts.

Johnny Cash blared from the loudspeakers. Andrej was almost out of money, and what he had done with it left him unsatisfied. Betting on greyhound races was not a good idea; you had to be an insider with know-how. A casino offered a more level playing field. What was stopping him from hitting up Tudjman for one more payoff? After all, he had already taken the first step; a follow-up claim would make no difference at all, morally speaking, and he could once again enjoy that blissful feeling of independence. A trip to Monte Carlo was naturally out of the question, but he could certainly have a go at the roulette tables in Rijeka. How much should he demand? At least as much as the first time, for sure. Tudjman could afford it, he had his pension and the income from the cable car. And what's more, last Saturday he had spotted him at the bus stop again, this time not holding a bunch of flowers, but a valise. Later, Andrej had checked the timetable and had reached the conclusion that Tudjman was waiting for the bus to Zagreb. And with a wife and half-witted daughter at home, at that. His warning had apparently not yet had its desired effect: Tudjman continued to carry on with his adulterous affair.

Above the blue hills in the distance, he could see the white trails of the airplanes heading to Athens.

He had a sudden brain wave. It was unconscionable that so much money was being spent on an over-the-hill, bleached-blonde slut from the big city while he, Andrej, could spend a fraction of that amount—he thought of what cash he had left—on something sensible and beneficial.

He went over to the shed and pulled open the sliding door. Inside, it was dark and stiflingly hot, and stank of dog excrement and gasoline. The fat man had taken off his leather jacket and was holding a baseball bat; another Gypsy held on to Laika, her skinny torso clamped between his legs and her forelegs pulled back so that her head lay helplessly on the hitch of an open trailer, in which Andrej saw four dead greyhounds. It was, simply, a chopping block.

"Stop!" he said. "I'll buy her from you."

The fat Gypsy looked up suspiciously. "This one?" he asked. "Why?"

"Just because," Andrej said. "For my little girl."

"They're valuable as pets," said a woman in the background, who sat breastfeeding a baby on a stack of car tires. "Good natured and affectionate. I'd give a thousand dinars for one."

Laika's bugged-out eyes were now fixed on him, but that was perhaps only because she had heard a different voice. He did not think she realized the danger she was in. He knew so much more than she did.

"All right, then," Andrej said. "A thousand dinars."

Laika lay feebly in the crate above the front wheel of his bicycle, too weak to brace herself against the bumping and jostling as they rode down the country road past the salt ponds. In the end, something good came of his so-called unlawful deed after all. He had taken a helpless creature under his wing. It was, moreover, a fancy animal, the only greyhound in town—of this he was certain.

He cycled excitedly through the deserted streets of the outskirts and looked forward to the splash he would make as he rode through the town center with his greyhound up front. He waved to the women who stood chatting under the awnings of shops and kiosks, and made an apologetic gesture as he passed, as though to say he would explain later how he came to own such a fine dog. He was, as it were, taking Laika on a victory lap, and therefore chose a longer route home, first along the boulevard, where he stopped to chat with the ice cream vendor, and then across the People's Square, where he paused in the shadow of the former archducal palace, not only for the shade but because a group of tourists had just gathered there, and the children might like to pat Laika on the head.

When he passed the clock museum, he raised his hand at the men sitting across the street at Café Rubin, where, he knew, Josip Tudjman was a regular.

The second letter, too, was postmarked in Rijeka. The envelope contained a postcard of the casino, with the message typed on the back; judging from the ink smears from the roller on either side of the text, it had apparently been done on quite an old machine.

> LIFE IS EXPENSIVE. ESPECIALLY THE NICER THINGS. NEED 3000 DINARS 1 MORE TIME OTHERWISE YOU KNOW WHAT WILL HAPPEN JOSIP TUDJMAN. NEXT TIME YOU'LL GET THE NEGATIVES. UNDER SAME BLOCK SAME TIME MONDAY.

Josip read the note while transporting his first clients of the day, an elderly German couple, to the top. The husband had the look of an ex-military man.

Josip put the note in his inside breast pocket and stared at the second, oncoming car.

There were only three rails, the middle rail being used by both cars except at the spot where they passed each other halfway up the hill. Here, for a length of twenty-four meters, the route branched into a full-fledged double track. Usually he explained this example of technical ingenuity to his passengers, which often resulted in a tip. But this time he had other things on his mind.

He did not have another three thousand dinars to spare. And even if he did manage to scrape together that sum, maybe by borrowing it, this would not be the end of it. The whole tone and style of this new letter showed that the extortionist felt empowered and imagined himself invincible: this was only the beginning. That postcard of the casino was a deliberate taunt. He saw no way out. Even if he were to give up Jana, the light of his life, this would not stop. Those snapshots of them at the base of the monument would be his downfall. There was no way on earth he could explain this to his wife. The black-mailer undoubtedly knew how pathologically jealous she was; the entire town knew. The consequences did not bear thinking about. His wife would not only go at him tooth and nail, she would destroy his very existence. Katarina in a mental home, divorce, disgrace, alimony. War veteran or no, he would lose his job at the funicular, as he could no longer claim to be a "comrade of virtuous character."

He also knew that Jana, as loving and passionate as she was, had no desire to establish a life with him. She had said as much at the very beginning of their relationship. "We share the golden moments, my darling. I look forward to them and love making myself beautiful for you and being with you—because you are such a fascinating man and a war hero, too, and I have such respect for how you care for that difficult wife of yours and that poor child. But I have my life here in Zagreb, and you have yours . . ."

He had to prevent, at all costs, the bomb that had been placed under his life from exploding. Even if it cost him another three thousand dinars.

A few scrawny rabbits were scavenging in the gravel between the rails and froze when they were suddenly closed in by the passing cars. This was a daily occurrence, but they never did seem to get used to it.

"You see, Traudl? This is the *Ausweichstelle*—the passing loop," the uptight German passenger said. "Just like in Wiesbaden!"

This had also impressed Jana, how the two cars passed each other at the midpoint, and then proceeded on their shared tracks. She had said: "We're like this, too, Josip. We meet each other halfway, and then carry on, each in our own direction."

Jana was an extraordinary woman. Ever since the day she had ridden the cable car with him, he saw his work in a new light.

He would have to borrow the money before it was too late. And then take measures to safeguard his situation in the future.

"Sprechen Sie Deutsch?" the passenger asked when Josip opened the door. They had bought a return ticket, of course;

there was no other reasonable way to get back to town from the top of the hill.

"A bit," Josip answered.

"I fought up there in those hills, 1943," the man said. "*Wehrmacht*, you understand?"

"*Ja,*" Josip said.

"Those were the days. But you still understand German. It wasn't so bad after all, was it? Culture! Liberation from *der Serben.*"

"*Jawohl,*" Josip said.

"Hush now, Erich," the woman said, leading him in the direction of the monument. "You don't know if this gentleman . . ."

He refilled the water tank. No more than a cubic meter, for the other car had automatically drained its ballast as soon as it reached the lower station and would not carry any new passengers on its way back up. It was only necessary to fill it to its seven-cubic-meter capacity if the downward car was empty and the upward car was conveying its maximum capacity of twenty-four passengers. This happened only rarely, however, mostly on Republic Day in November, when hundreds of party leaders would gather at the monument to lay wreaths. After the ceremony there was, of course, no water ballast necessary, the descending car being sufficiently heavy with its full load of passengers wanting to go home. Josip sometimes had to exercise his authority to prevent the party functionaries from crowding into an overfull car. The braking system was fail-safe, but rules were rules.

While he was waiting for his passengers to return, he re-examined the postcard. Three thousand dinars. And that ominous, shameless sentence: NEXT TIME YOU'LL GET THE NEGATIVES. This only meant that after this payment another demand would be coming. And besides, those negatives didn't mean a thing: the man could have already made a whole batch of prints to use in the future.

Josip fantasized about what he would do to this bastard if he were to manage to unmask him. He imagined his blackmailer as a small, ratlike man, whom he could overpower despite his age.

After disconnecting the water conduit, he straightened his back and looked out over the blue sea and the town.

Somewhere down there, he was convinced, his adversary lived; for he knew about Josip's marriage, his work, his daily routine, and he knew the town. In his mind's eye Josip went through the lineup of small, ratlike men who might fit the bill. Antić, the shoemaker. Old Vucović, who worked as a waiter at the Hotel Esplanade. And that garbage collector, a Bosnian, he thought, but he did not know his name. Antić was so skittish and withdrawn that he hardly ever ventured outside the dark basement vault where he had his workshop; you would never associate him with the brazen message on the back of the postcard from Rijeka, let alone with the casino pictured on the front. The Bosnian was a primitive fellow, maybe even illiterate; that's why he worked as a garbageman. An unlikely candidate, although he might well be the type to come up with the idea of that concrete block at the side of the road. Vucović, now there's someone he might want to keep an eye on. After all, it wasn't much of a jump from a luxury hotel to a casino, and perhaps having contact with foreigners had sparked strange notions in him. But how was he to tackle it? Go to the bar on the esplanade, order a drink, look the old man in the eye, and make a threatening comment hinting the jig was up?

And he did not even know for sure if the blackmailer was a small, ratlike man. It could also be a fat slob. It could be anyone.

Josip mounted the front platform of the car, awaiting his passengers, and looked out over the town and the sea.

He had been born here. And here he had always lived, with the exception of the last years of the war. The three-rail track at his feet pointed like an arrow at the core of his existence, at this small city on the coast. He knew everything like the back of his hand: the domes of the Church of Saint Anastasia, the white statues on the archducal palace cornices, the TV antennas on the tile rooftops, the Turkish fort around which the ring road curved, the concrete apartment blocks on the gray hillside, the power lines, the long rows of boats moored along the boulevard, the elegant forest of masts in the marina, the bay with its two uninhabited rocky islands, the expansive sea where, in the distance, container ships and cruise ships regularly passed.

This was his city, it was where he grew up, and thanks to Jana in far-off Zagreb he was strong enough to endure the hell of his own household. He wouldn't want to live anywhere else. But somewhere in that labyrinth hid a monster who was out to ruin his life.

His passengers returned, and Josip set the funicular in motion. The German couple seated themselves on the bench directly behind him. They must be rich, he thought, for the woman's jewelry looked like real gold, and the man wore an expensive wristwatch with a link band.

While the man read to his wife from the free brochure—track length, elevation change, average gradient—Josip alternately fixed his gaze on the passing rails and stones, on the empty ascending car, and on the tree crowns and rooftops that rose toward them. The town closed around them until the only view was that of the approaching eaves of the lower station.

The Luftwaffe had bombed the town during the war, as the German seated behind him was well aware. As Oberleutnant he had seen the relief Stukas, the Luftwaffe's dive-bombers, fly over the mountains where his battalion had been stranded for days and had suffered substantial losses. The bombardment had so badly damaged the funicular that the Yugoslavian units could no longer be supplied with heavy weapons, and this had eventually led to the German breakthrough toward Senj.

"And during your very first furlough, we got engaged," his wife said.

"Ja, so war's, Schatzi."

Josip brought the car to a halt and opened the door for his passengers, studiously avoiding all eye contact. When they had alighted, the man, holding an apparently preplanned gratuity in his left hand, said, "But that's all water under the bridge, *nicht wahr?* Now we've come to your fine country as guests. *Traudl, machst du bitte ein Foto?"*

The woman, familiar with her husband's wishes, already had her modern compact camera at the ready. The German extended his right hand and exclaimed, "Today, we're friends! I thank you for the enjoyable trip."

Josip refused. No photos of him in uniform shaking hands with a former Wehrmacht officer.

"Ne, hvala," he said.

"I beg your pardon?" the German asked.

Josip said in Croatian that a bomb dropped by a Stuka had hit his mother's house, and that she was burned alive.

"Pardon?" the German asked again.

Josip said in German that a bomb dropped by a Stuka had hit his mother's house, and that she was burned alive.

Then he left the platform and closed the kiosk door behind him.

He hung the OUT OF SERVICE sign in the window, lowered the blinds, removed his jacket, and sank into the wooden swivel chair. He lay the postcard in front of him and stared at it, his head in his hands.

He had friends, but borrowing this kind of money from a friend meant you owed them some sort of explanation, and this, he felt, even if he did not mention her by name, would sully the love between him and Jana. And besides, how could he borrow money without knowing how or even if he could repay it? He did not want to be indebted to anyone.

He opened the bottom drawer of the desk. Behind the carton of Ronhills was a bottle of slivovitz. Josip held the first swig in his mouth for some time, as though the brandy's proximity to his brain might help him think more clearly.

What if he were to put a note under the concrete block, asking for an extension? This was at most a stopgap measure and could have catastrophic consequences. He took his keyring and, the brandy still in his mouth, pulled open a higher drawer, the one with the cashbox. But this was insanity. If he pilfered from the cash drawer—and anyway, its contents would fall far short of what he needed—he would lose his job for sure. He swallowed with his eyes closed. When he opened them he saw, through a gap in the blinds, the German couple sitting on a cement bench across the street in the shade of the plane trees. That chic gray Mercedes parked farther up must be theirs. The man sat hunched forward, his hands between his knees; Josip did not see his face, only the top of his old-man trilby hat. He appeared to be unwell. His wife had one hand on her purse and the other on his shoulder.

Say he were to enlist the Bosnian garbageman to keep an eye on the concrete block next Monday. He could inconspicuously pick up trash in the shoulder of the Nikole Zrinskog and make a note of any suspicious behavior. But the blackmailer would most likely wait until the coast was clear. That spot in the curve in the ring road had been well chosen: out of view from the monument and even from the surrounding buildings. Post someone at the Turkish fort, and ask him to take down the license plate numbers of every car that drove down the Zrinskog? And then what? Besides, the cheat could also approach the spot on foot, from another direction, for instance by climbing up the hill from the slums down by the salt marsh.

He had to pay, at least this time.

Behind him there was a tentative knock at the door. He bent forward and peered through the gap between the slats. The bench was empty, and the chic Mercedes was still there.

Josip put on his uniform jacket and opened the door.

It was the German couple.

"Yes?" he asked gruffly.

"*Bitte,*" the woman said gently. "Erich would very much like to . . ."

The man removed his lightweight hat and looked at him. His thin lips quivered.

"*Jako mi je žao,*" he said. *I apologize.* They must have looked it up in their *Langenscheidt Sprachführer*.

Josip did not reply, in part because the slivovitz had made him quite dizzy.

The German, tears in his light-blue eyes, launched into an explanation that Josip did not understand. He cast a woozy but stern glance at the woman, who at least spoke clearly. The matter became clearer when the man held out an envelope. The flap was open, revealing a thick wad of banknotes.

"Please accept it," said the woman. "It would mean a lot to us."

Josip hesitated, leaning against the doorframe, and struggled to process his bewilderment and conflicting emotions.

"Erich has a generous pension," the woman insisted. *"Bitte."*

He took the envelope, nodded, and said in Croatian, "Just this once." This was a strange answer, but he assumed they did not understand it.

He saluted, even though his uniform cap still lay on the desk, and quickly shut the kiosk door, cutting off the German man's thanks.

Eventually the Mercedes drove off, slowly and cautiously, spotted like a panther in the shadows of the plane trees.

Only then did Josip remove the banknotes from the envelope. Erich did indeed have a generous pension: it was more than ten thousand dinars.

Andrej flaunted his greyhound. He had bought a small red leather collar that contrasted nicely with her white coat. Laika slept in a laundry basket lined with a blanket. She slept more or less constantly, but as soon as Andrej moved or spoke, she would open her eyes. They were round, sad eyes; she looked at him with the expression of a terminally ill patient, surprised that anyone still cared about her. When she wasn't sleeping, she trembled. She often even trembled in her sleep. But soon enough it became clear that there was nothing at all wrong with her. The first time he let her free on the small beach beyond the boulevard wall, she stood quaking next to him. Andrej gestured and coaxed her encouragingly, but she stuck close to his heels, her back arched. They were a curious-looking pair: a man more than two meters tall and a slight, skinny greyhound. He bent over and picked up something to throw, the first thing he could find, a clump of dried seaweed. Laika took off like a shot and raced under the airborne seaweed before it landed. A small group of children up on the boulevard started clapping and shouting.

"Any of you have a ball?" Andrej shouted.

A little girl held up an orange ball.

Andrej hooked a finger under Laika's collar and instructed them what to do; the children ran past the palm trees, a good hundred meters along the boulevard.

"Now!" Andrej roared, gesturing broadly with his free arm. They threw the ball onto the beach, and at the same time he released Laika. She tore after the ball like a white bolt of lightning. Andrej trotted after her.

"Wow," shouted one boy. "She sure is fast! Is that a real racing dog, mister?"

"Yes," Andrej said, petting Laika's narrow head. "A real English racing dog. I bought her in London."

"Can she run faster than a horse?" the girl asked.

"Of course. Much faster."

"Faster than a car?"

"Count on it. She's the fastest dog in the world."

"Faster than a train, too?"

Andrej did not answer. He grasped his dog's ears and turned her head toward a small group of pelicans that had assembled at the water's edge in the distance.

"See those animals there, girl? D'you see those ugly pink creatures?" He moved her silky ears up and down as though they were wings. "Chase them away. Go!"

She shot down the beach, reaching her top speed before the pelicans saw her coming and set off in unison in a gait not much clumsier than that of Andrej himself, who had run down the beach after her. Then they spread their wings and lifted off, while Laika stood barking, her legs spread and her back arched. It looked like a huge effort; with each high-pitched yelp her body contracted so fiercely that she nearly toppled over.

"Well done, girl," Andrej panted. Laika looked at him with her round eyes as though to say: "Why didn't you just say so in the first place."

The pelicans circled, landed together like heavy seaplanes a safe distance from the beach, and from there kept a close eye on the peculiar beach walker and his dog.

On their way home, Laika ran in big ovals and figure-eights around her master. He bought her a can of salmon.

Josip had put the three thousand dinars under the concrete block, with a note saying that this was absolutely the last time, and that he wanted the negatives. He had spent the rest of Erich's money entirely on pleasurable things. He took Jana out and gave her a gold bracelet. He bought a new jigsaw puzzle for his daughter, of Saint Peter's in Rome. He had wanted to buy a digital watch for himself, but in the end decided he should buy a present for his wife.

It had been years since they gave each other gifts, so Katarina believed she was the only one in the family who ever had a birthday.

When he presented his wife with a color television, she grabbed it, box and all, and carried it to her bedroom.

"Shall I hook it up for you?" he asked. "It's got a room antenna."

She gaped at him like a Mongolian empress who had just learned of a plot against her life and slammed the door in his face.

His daughter, drooling, dumped the thousand puzzle pieces of Saint Peter's onto the rug and exclaimed, "Come on, Papa!"

Andrej blew his money within a matter of hours, thanks to just one ill-conceived wager; at one point he had chips worth ten thousand dinars piled up before him. He felt he was on his way to becoming a first-class player and deserved a second chance. So he would wait a month or so and then cash in on Tudjman one last time. After that he would let him be. Andrej even considered sharing the winnings with him, if he were to hit the jackpot at the casino. He would give him, together with the negatives and the remaining prints, a sum of money as a sort of compensation. Signed, *Your Unknown Friend.* But first he needed another few thousand dinars.

Things were going his way, and he felt heartened. The postal workers' union had offered him a position—unpaid, admittedly, but an honor nonetheless. The steaming open of envelopes, too, became increasingly profitable. Prudently, of course—letters from fellow townsmen employed as migrant workers in Germany, he left alone; registered letters were likewise sacred. But if a granny abroad was so stupid and stingy as to enclose money with a birthday card to her granddaughter, and not send it registered—well, that was fair game. No one could prove that he had ever laid eyes on that missing letter.

With Laika curled up in her basket and him seated at the kitchen table sorting the mail, he felt like a monarch who decided which tributes from subjugated nations he would let pass. It was up to him, Andrej, to decide who received mail, and who did not. He was particularly merciless regarding mail addressed to guests at the Hotel Esplanade. These he often threw away, especially if they were written in a language he did not understand. He saw it, in a sense, as an act of patriotism.

44

PART 2

It was March and the pelicans had not yet returned. They must be very picky creatures, for while there were perhaps warmer regions elsewhere, nowhere was more pleasant and beautiful than here. The days were not as hot as in summer, the nights cool but no longer chilly. The town lay charmingly on the bay, basking in an almost timeless beauty and watching over the to-and-fro of fishing boats and motorized yachts on the blue sea, the way an older lady who once waltzed with the young emperor Franz Josef might now observe the young people sashaying about the dance floor. There were hardly any tourists at this time of year, and in a way, it was nice not to have to share one's familiar haunts with strangers. Now it was mostly the youths from the concrete apartment blocks up the hill who came to the old town center, often on sputtering motor scooters, in search of diversion not available in their parts, for only here did you have cafés and grillrooms, and even an arcade with slot machines. Belgrade had recently gotten the first-ever McDonald's in a Communist country, but the capital was too far away.

Josip sat, as he did every Saturday, at an outdoor table at Café Rubin with a glass of beer. Around him, as usual, were friends, neighbors, and former comrades. Men whom he could turn to for help if he saw no other way out. The blackmailer was still demanding money, now even twice as much as at first. The last note included a snapshot he had apparently been saving up: Josip between Jana's legs.

Even if he were prepared to pay, his funds had dried up. He would have to borrow money. Or consult someone more strong minded than himself, with other methods of settling the matter. Sitting next to him was Marković, the bus driver. He drank cola, as it was nearly time for his shift. A heavyset man who always wore a nappa vest and smelled of garlic. Josip and he were not good friends, and besides, he was a simpleton and didn't earn enough to be able to give Josip a loan. The pharmacist Knević, on the other hand, was well off, but he was a know-it-all who believed it was his right to pontificate on world events on behalf of the entire café. Not someone Josip wanted to be indebted to. Schmitz, the owner of the photography studio, might be a possibility: he was good natured and cooperative. The problem with Schmitz was that he had collaborated with the Germans during the war and was incorrigibly anti-Semitic. Each of the men at the café had his own wartime past. All these things had been put to rest—in such a small town there was no other choice—and Schmitz had made the photo albums of his wedding, but still, Josip could not imagine taking a man like him into his confidence.

The sun set, searching for ever larger gaps in the foliage of the plane trees on the square, while Knević held forth on the American presidential elections and predicted a victory for Dukakis.

The only one left was Mario. A fellow partisan and comrade, back in the day. They even shared the exact same birth date. Mario was his brother-in-law and best friend; Josip had helped him build his house up on the hillside, just to the north of the funicular. For weeks, Josip laid bricks, dug trenches for the plumbing, and together they had laid the granite bathroom floor. Regrettably, they had drifted apart of late. Perhaps the disparity between their lives had become too great: the one was successful in business and happily married, the other struggled to make ends meet and had a miserable homelife. It shouldn't be so, but developments like these inevitably undermine the sense of equality on which all friendships are based.

Josip kept his sunglasses on, although the sun had now gone down, and listened to Mario tell a long and doubtless completely fabricated story about Swiss boarding-school girls. Mario fancied himself God's gift to women, even though he had long been happily married to the sister of Josip's wife. No one believed that he had had more than a thousand women, as he was wont to claim; in any case, he was physically an improbable Don Juan, with his potbelly and balding head.

Mario was a childish fantasist. Josip would always be fond of him, perhaps even more than of himself. This was exactly why he did not want to ask Mario for money, even though he knew his brother-in-law would lend him whatever he asked for; they had shared only good times, and he simply couldn't embroil him in this dirty business.

The bus that Marković would soon be taking over pulled in across the square.

When it comes down to it, Josip mused as he drank the rest of his tepid beer, you're on your own. He was disappointed in his friends, in Mario, too, now that it was clear he couldn't ask any of them for help.

Andrej the postman cycled past, as always erect on the saddle and in full uniform, cap and all.

"Strange fellow," Knević pronounced. "I hear he's in the union. A Serbian snake pit—what business does a Croatian have there? Nothing but vain ambition, if you ask me."

"Wasn't much of a soccer player, either," Marković added.

Andrej rested his bicycle on its kickstand, opened the flap of his saddlebag, took out a packet, and walked over to the entrance of the clock museum, balancing the packet at shoulder height on the fingertips of his right hand.

"Look at that, will you," Marković said. "Thinks he's a pastry chef carrying a tart."

"A strange bird, that's for sure," Knević said. "Maybe he's a homosexual."

"I don't think so," said Josip, who knew how keen on movie stars and princesses Andrej was.

"So why isn't he married?" the pharmacist asked.

"Just too timid, poor guy," Mario said, and got up to go to the restroom.

"He does have some artistic talent," said Schmitz in his defense. "Those postcards of the butterflies still sell well."

The postman came out of the museum and remounted his bicycle. Josip's sunglasses blotted out much of the usual tableau the town square offered, with its view of the museum's clock tower, built in some Italian style or other. He sat slouched in a plastic chair and pondered ordering another glass of beer, as he had no desire whatsoever to return home. Anywhere was better than home.

Through the tinted lenses, the world was simplified into a violet sky, and the dark rest. Josip was satisfied with that. Especially now that the dark rest became even larger because of the bus that had stopped just in front of the café.

The ambient sounds also receded; he had all but stopped listening.

Until he heard the sudden thud. He looked up and saw, between the streaks of light caused by the scratches on his sunglasses, a dark figure sail through the air, a completely improbable postman arched like a pole vaulter above an invisible crossbar. Josip yanked off his sunglasses, there was a second thud, and Andrej slid sideways off the hood of a car.

The others leapt up, but Josip needed a few moments to put the world back into focus. The car that had hit Andrej was just passing the parked bus. The Volkswagen he landed on, smashing its windshield, was parked in front of an ATM and facing against the traffic. Andrej lay on his belly, arms and legs spread as though he were trying to hold back the large pool of blood that was spreading out from under him. Car doors opened, people shouted. The bus let out a pneumatic hiss, like a prehistoric monster that regarded the mangled bicycle on the ground as a kind of alien insect.

Marković rushed over, a woman turned her child's stroller on its back wheels and hurried off in the opposite direction. Despite all the commotion, Josip had the sensation of everything happening in slow motion. Chair legs scraped the pavement, Schmitz and the pharmacist got up, a startled Mario appeared in the doorway.

"Call an ambulance!" Josip called to him.

The blood had two colors, dark and light red, which mixed like when a river empties into the sea. Andrej was covered in shards of safety glass. The man at the ATM looked over his shoulder but waited until he could retrieve his bank card. Josip knelt alongside Andrej.

"The ambulance is on its way," Mario said.

"Arterial bleeding," Josip said. "We have to turn him over."

They did what they had done half a lifetime ago, before the postman was even born, whenever a comrade was hit by shrapnel: Mario lifted the victim's torso, they carefully removed his jacket, and Josip tied a tourniquet—his necktie with the funicular's emblem—just under the armpit and pulled it as tightly as he could. The bleeding stopped, but Andrej was still unconscious.

The ambulance, its siren wailing and lights revolving, arrived surprisingly quickly, but was blocked some thirty meters back by the bus, cars, and the mangled bicycle. The paramedics came to assess the situation and returned to get a stretcher.

"Move that damn bus!" Josip snarled at Marković, who just stood there gawking.

"Can't," said the pharmacist. "The police haven't arrived yet."

Andrej lay there peacefully, as though he were soaking up all the attention. The trickle of blood running down his long chin gave him the look of a bon vivant who couldn't be bothered to use his napkin.

Sixteen arms lifted him onto the stretcher, and the ambulance backed down the street, lights and siren still going, until it was able to turn.

"There was nothing I could do," said the driver of the car that had hit him.

"Shut your trap, man!" Marković barked and grabbed him. "Tell that to the cops. You should've waited behind the bus! Behind the bus, you get it? In America they'd give you the electric chair! There could've been children crossing. Children, you get it?"

"Let's be reasonable, this isn't a no-passing zone," said Knević, the pharmacist.

"But it *is* a no-parking zone," Marković said, now taking the owner of the Volkswagen by the arm, as if to hinder an escape attempt. "And facing the traffic flow, at that. What business did you have stopping your car there, eh? And besides, I've never seen you before. You're not from here, are you?"

"My wife's birthday is tomorrow . . . I only wanted to . . ."

"Tell that to the cops," Marković said, still tightly holding the man's arm.

The sun had set, and Josip had a good excuse for not returning home yet.

They eventually gave their statements to the police, and then he, Mario, Schmitz, Marković, and the pharmacist discussed what should be done with Andrej's mangled bicycle, his cap and jacket, and the still-full mailbags.

Mario offered to take Andrej's belongings to his apartment on the harbor—his keys were still in the uniform pocket—and to look after his dog. In the days thereafter, Josip would take over, and if he did not have the time, Schmitz would fill in.

When it was Josip's turn, he found the semi-basement apartment to be a typical bachelor pad, although in a way it was homier than his own house. There was even a vase of lilacs on the Formica-topped kitchen table. The dog cocked its head warily as Josip fastened the leash. When they got back, he looked through the kitchen cabinets for dog food and found seven oval tins of salmon and a box of dry food. Apparently this was her menu.

He unconsciously took in the apartment. Long woolen socks hung on a clothes-drying rack, and Andrej had quite an expensive-looking Kodak. That must be what he used to take those butterfly shots on the postcards.

Josip emptied the undelivered mail from the saddlebags into a plastic bag. He would inform the postal service so that they could pick it up at his kiosk tomorrow.

He noticed that one side pocket contained opened envelopes. That was strange. He took one out and gave it a closer look. British postage stamp, addressed to Joyce Kimberley, c/o Hotel Esplanade. There was a letter in it, which, despite his poor English, Josip could follow: . . . *sorry to hear about your troubles . . . hope you notified your bank about those Eurocheques . . . take care . . . hope this £50 will help . . . Love, Daddy.*

Fifty pounds was a huge sum of money. Josip searched the other open envelopes and determined that there were probably others that had contained money. From an aunt to her niece on her birthday, from a man who apologized for returning a borrowed car with an almost-empty tank. These were in

Serbo-Croatian, so the amounts would probably have been in dinars, and not very much.

Josip leaned back.

The dog now lay flat in its laundry basket; only a single bent ear stuck out above the rim.

The barred window was open, he heard gulls screeching, men talking, the rattling wheels of a cart.

He folded his hands, put them on his balding head, and thought.

In the end, because he was not satisfied with his thoughts and because this was not a position a person could hold for long, he let his arms drop to his sides.

Andrej's bloodied uniform jacket was draped over the back of the chair where he was sitting, and his hand slid, as though it were his own jacket, down over the fabric.

Then he patted the inside breast pocket, slowly pulled out the wallet, and flipped it open. It contained, in addition to a goodly sum in dinars, a fifty-pound note with Queen Elizabeth on the front.

"Your master is a bad man," he said to the bitch, who raised her head and regarded him dejectedly. "He is a thief. A criminal. I hadn't expected that of him."

Andrej would no longer be needing the mailbags, nor his uniform jacket or his cap with the emblem with stylized wings, he thought, so he would turn them all over in one go when the postal service van came.

But on the other hand, it was mean to lodge a criminal complaint against a man who might at this very moment be lying in a coma.

He decided to keep the compromising articles—the opened letters and the banknote—and when Andrej got out of the hospital, he would take it from there.

He filled Laika's water bowl and stroked her head.

"I'll be back tomorrow," he said. "Nothing you can do about it, is there?"

She watched him leave, her eyes bulging, her narrow head resting on the edge of the basket. For Laika, life was pure stress.

Josip took Laika out every day, for Mario had a busy job and a large family. When the tins of salmon ran out, he bought new ones. He always kept her on the leash because he had no experience with dogs and was afraid she might run away. Laika appeared to interpret this as a punishment, and whenever he looked down at her she hurried to his other side, with a gait somewhere between slinking and scampering. She was afraid of him, that much was clear, although he had no idea why.

On his day off he took her on a somewhat longer walk, up to the concrete block on the Ulica Zrinskog. A week earlier he had put, instead of an envelope of money, a note under the rock asking for an extension. Strangely enough, the note was still there. Josip hesitated. Had the blackmailer left it there intentionally, as a sign he wasn't buying it? In any case, he hadn't made another move yet. Josip's wife ranted and raved as always, but nothing indicated she had any knowledge of his liaison.

She scoffed at his explanations when he left town for a few days. A chess tournament, a refresher course at the railways, an invented doctor's appointment. Her theory was unshakable: whenever her husband was out of sight, he was cheating on her. There was no arguing with it.

He always mentioned places other than Zagreb—the name of the city alone was sacred to him—but this was a moot point, as she was incapable of taking action. She was nearly illiterate, and if she left the house at all she never went farther than the corner drugstore, and the neighborhood women avoided her. Her inability to deal with reality was torture for him, but at the same time it guaranteed that he was free to come and go as he pleased.

Laika took advantage of the stop to squat and relieve herself. As always, she looked at him with scared, bugged-out eyes, which bulged even more from the effort of emptying her bowels. She never turned her back to him, as though she feared some unforeseen assault.

"Good girl," he said, and looked around before taking the envelope of money from his inside pocket. He had exchanged the fifty-pound note. There was no one around; crickets chirped, the Yugoslavian flag hung slackly on the fort's flagpole, the sea was still and blue, with only a ripple here and there brought on by a breeze that died out before reaching land.

Josip lifted one edge of the block, removed his note, and slid the envelope with the money underneath.

"There," he said to the dog, "now he'll leave us in peace for a while."

Laika's drooping tail swished halfheartedly—one could hardly call it wagging.

Josip's pace became almost jaunty as he walked back down to the old city, and Laika trotted alongside him, a bit more blithely than usual.

He had made a decision. He had found the solution. He did not need to borrow money from his friends.

He impulsively decided to take Laika home with him, regardless of what his wife would say. Things there couldn't get any worse than they already were, and maybe Katarina would be amused. After all, his inspiration was thanks to the dog.

He tied her to the Alka-Seltzer sign that Knević placed on the sidewalk in front of his pharmacy every day and went inside to ask how the postman was faring.

He was in stable condition, said Knević, who, more or less as the envoy of the café regulars, had visited him in the hospital. Concussion, fractured collarbone and arm, facial wounds, significant blood loss.

"They've given him four transfusions. Maybe even with his own blood—did you know he was a donor?"

No, Josip did not know that.

"He had one of those medallions around his neck, with his blood type. That might have saved his life."

"A good man, then, our Andrej. I had no idea he donated blood."

"He did it for the money," Knević said.

"Of course, that's true, isn't it. Do you know when he'll be discharged?"

"They usually keep you in for two weeks. But he insists on getting out earlier, the sooner the better. When he came to, his first words were, 'Home . . . the mail . . . the mail . . .'"

"Utter dedication," Josip said, deadpan.

When he arrived home with the dog, his wife was sitting in the kitchen smoking, a full ashtray and a pack of cigarettes within arm's reach.

"Hello," he said. He hadn't called her by her name in years. "We've got a guest. I've brought her for Katarina."

Now, like whenever he spoke to her in a firm, dispassionate tone, she did not reply, but stared at him blankly. Her face, once attractive, albeit somewhat peasantish, had become round and contourless, as though she originated on the distant Asian steppes rather than a village not even fifty kilometers away; it looked like her mental degradation was accompanied by the sudden manifestation of the genes of God knows which Mongolian or Kyrgyz tribe. Josip had not only lost the young woman he once loved, but he was condemned to a life with a creature with whom, he felt at times, he did not even share a common race or even species. In spite of all this he tended to treat her with courtesy and respect, but she only took this as a sign of weakness and attacked him mercilessly. Only when, like now, he assumed a posture that would not abide dissent did she retreat into passivity. Severity and hard-nosedness were all she responded to. Unfortunately this was not in his nature, and he could not maintain it constantly. She looked at him in silence, like a kulak awaiting her master's cudgel. Saliva glistened on her chin.

"I want you to let her enjoy it. No scenes. Understood?"

She gaped at him with her vacant blue eyes, hands folded on her lap, her only response being to stick her foot in the drum of the washing machine, as though expecting a pedicure.

Josip held the leash so tightly that the dog began to make rasping sounds. His wife kept quiet, but she was as unpredictable as a proletarian on the eve of the revolution. Sometimes he was afraid she would slit his throat while he slept.

He went to his bedroom, Katarina's favorite place to play. He cracked open the door and used his leg to keep the dog out

61

of sight, for it had to be a surprise. She was sitting cross-legged on the rug next to the bed, working on her pony puzzle.

"Sweetheart? Can I come in?" This was a joke that always got a laugh; she grinned, gurgled some strange noises, and batted wildly at the air with her outstretched arms, as though to say, "Yes, yes, now the fun can start."

"We've got an important visitor. A princess."

Katarina pulled her dress over her knees and waited. He undid the leash and pushed Laika inside.

Laika strode across the rug as only a creature on four greyhound legs could and seated herself with unassuming gracefulness. Katarina laid the puzzle pieces still in her hand carefully onto the rug. Laika cocked her narrow head and followed Katarina's every move. Katarina reached out and touched the dog's nose. Laika looked at her with bulging eyes, cautiously raised a foreleg, and placed it on the girl's knee. They both drooled.

Josip took off his jacket and unbuttoned his shirt.

"You'll be friends, won't you?"

"Yes," said Katarina thoughtfully, "I'm fluzzie number one and she's fluzzie number hundred."

"That's nice. Now Papa's going to lie down on the bed. Papa's tired."

Josip stared at the ceiling fan, which for some thirty years had been as inert as a grave cross. It was a good plan. He would let one criminal pay the other. A win-win situation: Andrej could keep his job, the blackmailer would get his money, and he himself would get off scot-free.

But how and where to arrange the payoffs?

While he stared at the motionless blades of the fan and at the flies creeping over them, he came up with an absurd idea.

Couldn't he pick out another concrete block at the side of the ring road, so that the criminals actually paid each other, without him as intermediary? That would be a nifty trick, and one with a fine moral.

Josip started to laugh. First noiselessly, but then with long, rasping, deep breaths that made his belly shake.

Katarina's eyeglassed head poked over the edge of the bed.

"Why are you laughing?" she said. "You never laugh."

"Yes, I know," Josip replied, and made himself more comfortable by undoing the top button of his trousers.

"So why?"

Now half a worried greyhound head also poked over the edge of the bed.

"That's a secret. I'll tell you another time."

"Stupid Papa," she shouted angrily. His daughter did not like it when things were not as they usually were. The last time he returned from Zagreb, she had sniffed him suspiciously and said, "You smell too sweet." In the future he would take a shower before getting on the bus.

"Go work on your puzzle," he said.

Right now he had to think practically. He could simply address the letter to Andrej and put it in the mail; the postman would deliver it to himself, once he was better. He would never ask for more money than the blackmailer demanded from him. He was a decent man, after all. A concrete block at the side of the Zrinskog as a drop-off point was by now a tried-and-true method, but it seemed to him better to pick his own spot. In his mind's eye he traversed the city, starting on the boulevard and then up through the old town, each time via a different alley or stairway. But he mustn't choose somewhere too close to home. The new apartment blocks up on the hill were not an option, as this was entirely unfamiliar terrain. It wasn't at all easy to think like a criminal when you weren't one.

With each piece of the jigsaw puzzle, his daughter explained to Laika in great detail what she was doing. The dog in turn made the occasional squeaking noise, which he hoped did not mean she needed to be taken out.

Little by little, his thoughts brought him higher up in the hills, and farther outside town. The lookout from the funicular's upper station offered him myriad possibilities. Wasn't there, a bit to the north, a narrow, steep stretch of farmland and a few vineyards? He had seldom been there but could picture it quite clearly now. There were narrow paths and dirt roads, rising and falling but always more or less following the contour lines. There were uninhabited huts and sheds where landholders or tenant farmers stored their tractors and equipment. The earth was red-brown and arid, and when it was plowed, the furrows traced patterns in the landscape resembling fingerprints. The grapes grown there were of such poor quality that they were used only for vinegar or the very cheapest supermarket wine sold in paper cartons. This was a promising place for the beginning blackmailer: it was off the beaten track, and he could walk there from the heroes' monument unseen. Now Josip remembered the overhead power lines. Aside from the army's broadcasting mast on a hilltop farther to the north, these were the region's highest structures. Although he understood nothing of electrotechnology, he had always liked them, probably because they were so simply and transparently constructed, as though from a Meccano set; like three acrobats standing on each other's shoulders, their stumpy metal arms spread wide and escorting the eighteen thick cables in elegant catenaries up the hillside until they disappeared behind the limestone peaks. Josip clearly imagined the entire setting. But what now interested him most—the base of each tower—escaped him. He would have to visit the place to take a closer look. If he remembered correctly, farmers plowed around the concrete corner blocks that supported the pylons, and in between them grew a wild patch of impenetrable thornbushes. That would be the ideal drop-off spot.

Josip suddenly felt incredibly talented, lying there on his bed and working out the details of a game he had never played before. "Papa, can she come live with us?" asked his daughter.

"Who?" he asked absently.

"The doggy."

"I don't think so, honey. She belongs to the postman, and one of these days he'll get out of the hospital and he'll be wanting her back."

"Maybe he won't get out, ever," Katarina said hopefully. "Maybe he'll die."

"Don't say things like that. It's not nice. And besides, the postman is a good friend of mine."

"Why?"

"Because I helped save his life. That makes you friends with the person, you see?"

His daughter did not answer, but he could tell she was sulking.

What had steered Andrej onto the road to vice? Perhaps being a bachelor. Josip had always thought it strange, his fascination with those magazines—even the foreign ones he couldn't read, as long as they featured pictures of glamorous women. He must be so lonely. He had no Jana in his life.

Josip's mind wandered to his next visit to Zagreb, the following week already. There was nothing finer in life than Jana's nylon-clad thighs. He wondered why she never became a film star. He had never experienced moments of greater bliss than on her sofa, after she had put on some soft jazz and dimmed the brass lamps with the pink lampshades. He hadn't even known that dimmers existed until he met Jana. At home the light switches were all black Bakelite rotary knobs, which you dared not touch with damp hands. Of course, the gifts he gave her played a role, but the bottom line was true love. He considered himself fortunate that life had granted him the kind of happiness poor Andrej would never know.

Andrej left the hospital earlier than the doctors had wanted and went straight home. The bunch of wildflowers had wilted, and the vase was dry. Laika wasn't there. Knević had told him Schmitz, Mario, and Tudjman had taken turns caring for her. Tudjman, of all people. Andrej's uniform jacket lay folded on the kitchen table, still in the plastic cover from the dry cleaners, the cap resting on top. At first glance it did not look like his malfeasance had been discovered. Even the empty mailbags hung over the back of a chair, like saddlebags awaiting a fresh horse so as to resume their journey. The bicycle was gone, of course; it had most likely been totaled. That day's mail would certainly have long been delivered by a colleague. But what about those letters he had steamed open? There was no memo of dismissal from the postal service, no letter from the postal workers' union offering legal aid, no court subpoena.

Andrej stumbled, his head still bandaged, through the apartment looking for clues. Nothing appeared to have been touched—until he opened his wallet, which had been placed meticulously on a corner of the kitchen table, as though the finder was keen to emphasize that his privacy had been thoroughly respected.

The amount in dinars, which he remembered precisely, was still there. But one thing was missing: the British banknote.

Andrej telephoned the postmaster, who expressed his surprise that he wanted to get back to work so soon. Why not take six or ten weeks' rest after this occupational injury? Why not take advantage of the fully paid physical rehab he was entitled to? But Andrej did not want rehab. He wanted to know who had been snooping in his mailbags that day, who had taken the banknote from his wallet. That very first evening he took a walk along the ring road. Tudjman's envelope containing the thousand-dinar notes was still under the concrete block. That proved, at least, that even though he'd been in Andrej's apartment to care for the dog, Tudjman hadn't connected him with the blackmail. Apparently he hadn't looked in the cabinet where Andrej kept the photos and negatives.

The next day he went to the pharmacy to pick up blood thinners and sleeping pills, and casually inquired who had given him first aid at the scene of the accident.

"Oh . . . ," Knević said, "everyone rushed to help. We were all sitting there when it happened."

"Yes, yes, that saved my life. But afterward? I mean, who took my uniform to the dry cleaners? And who turned the undelivered mail over to the postmaster? I want to thank everyone personally."

"Tudjman took care of the dog, mostly. He offered to right away," Knević said, sliding a paper bag with handles across the counter as he started to instruct Andrej on the use of the injection needles for the blood thinners.

"I know. And the mail, and my personal belongings?"

"Gosh, I couldn't say. Everyone was crowded around . . . Mario, maybe? Or no, it might have been Marković, he was going to take your mailbags on the bus. I really can't remember, to be honest."

"Not Schmitz?"

"No, not him. He did offer to finish your round, but you know how much trouble he has walking, especially on stairs."

"Yes . . . so you think it was Marković?"

"I didn't say that. Why don't you just come down to Café Rubin sometime? We're there every Saturday afternoon, at the tables out front. You could offer a thank-you round, if you want. Everyone did their bit."

"Good idea! I'll do that," Andrej said.

But first he went in search of Marković, whom he found tinkering with a moped.

"A beaut, isn't it? For my daughter. She'll be turning sixteen in a few days."

"Sure is," Andrej said, letting himself be hugged and clapped on the back. "Careful, my shoulder . . ."

"How are you? All patched up? You were always injury prone, if I remember, and of course you shouldn't go riding into moving cars."

Marković had been a midfielder for Dinamo, the team for which Andrej, for lack of anyone better, had been made goalkeeper.

"Can you help me get this thing up on the stand? The back wheel's wobbling."

"I can try."

"I'll lift it," Marković said, taking off his nappa jacket, "you just slide it underneath. There we are. *To je gotovo.*"

He fumbled in his toolbox in search of the right wrench. "She'll love it. A real Simson Schwalbe. Usually only the college students in Berlin and Zagreb ride these."

"Nice color, too, that green," Andrej muttered. "Say, Marković . . ."

"Yeah?" he said, a cotter pin clamped between his teeth.

"Did you take my mailbags with you that day?"

"Me? How do you mean?" Marković asked as he wriggled the back wheel off the axle.

"I'd put something personal in the side pocket, and thought that if you had found it . . ."

"Nope. I had my bus route to do, so I couldn't also be worrying about your things. I did hold on to that guy with the illegally parked Volkswagen until the police arrived."

"Yes, I heard. Well done, man. But do you know who did take my mailbags?"

"No idea," Marković said, sitting on the driveway, legs spread and the wheel on his knees. "Schmitz, maybe. He offered to finish your route. Lame old Schmitz, of all people! He needs a cane just to hoist himself up off the toilet. Look at that, will you, I'm going to have to replace all these spokes."

"Schmitz? Not Tudjman?"

"Haven't the foggiest," replied the bus driver. "Why don't you ask them? Drop by any Saturday afternoon, everyone who was there will be at the café then."

"I'll do that, for sure."

Andrej sat at the harbor for over an hour. He had treated himself to an ice cream sandwich and threw the last bits of the wafer into the water. After licking off the wrapper, he tossed this, too, into the water, watching as the silver foil slowly disappeared, surrounded by a school of tiny fish. Just like a sinking shipwreck gets attacked by sharks, he thought.

The metal of the mooring bollard on which he sat was agreeably warm, and he was in no hurry to resume his pursuit. Better to think things through first. Old Schmitz was certainly an odd bird, but he was a charitable fellow; you'd never suspect him of stealing money. He had to be clever about broaching the subject, so that Schmitz would not catch on and would perhaps point him in the right direction.

The ferry from Ancona, which served the town on a weekly basis during the summer months, and in low season just once a month, was approaching the dock at the far end of the boulevard. It was a massive white vessel with tall smokestacks, and it always attracted a lot of attention. The ice cream man started pushing his cart toward the dock; the hotel, the restaurants, and the owners of vacation bungalows would be sending pitchmen armed with brochures and business cards—doubtless in vain, because aside from the trucks only a few cars drove over the apron ramp, and these were mostly en route to somewhere else and only used the ferry because of its handy and affordable connection from Italy.

Andrej, too, often went to watch, in the hope of catching a glimpse of the newest model Lancia or Ford, but he could spot them from where he now sat.

He wore white shorts and a white short-sleeved shirt, which, together with the white bandage around his head and his tall posture, gave him an exotic, maybe even princely, air. And indeed, it looked as though he were holding court; townsfolk came over, one after the other, to congratulate him on his recovery, even people whom he didn't think knew him. An older woman pulling a plaid wheeled shopping cart stopped and said she hoped he would soon be delivering her mail again, because it just wasn't the same when someone else did it. A tanned, wiry old man who rented out his fishing boat for day trips came over and shook his hand. Andrej was getting more attention than ever, and he soaked it up. It was as if the town finally recognized him as a truly singular local son. Were it not for the unanswered conundrum of the missing envelopes and the fifty-pound note he might have been completely happy. The sky was blue and cloudless; only the faraway southern horizon was hazy, auguring rain. A small group of pelicans, apparently just arrived from Africa, stood stock still and stared vacantly into space, fortunately not too close by. The cable car was stationary, too, the car up top on the right-hand side. Josip Tudjman was a man of habit. Andrej had placed his sandaled right foot against a hawser that stretched to a floating dock, to which a row of small motorboats was moored. The rope tautened and slacked with the gentle swell of the water in the bay, making it look like he was operating the foot pedal of a huge nautical organ. A boy in a Pioneer's uniform, complete with blue cap and red neckerchief, approached. Like Andrej, he wore short pants. The boy saluted and said: "Hello, mister, where's your dog?"

"You know my dog?" asked Andrej, smiling.

"Sure I do. The English racing dog. We threw the orange ball for her that time, remember? But of course, that was before I took the Pioneer's oath. Now I'm my troop guide."

"Good for you, son. What's your name?"

"Mirko, sir."

"That's a fine name. And when did you take your oath?"

"Last year already, sir. We stand firmly behind the ideals of our Socialist Republic! *Smrt fašizmu!*"

"Attaboy! I did my part, too."

"Were you in the Great Patriotic War?"

"No, I'm not your grandpa! But I was a striker for the national soccer team, when we played in the World Cup."

Lies, in a way, are so much more personal than the truth, Andrej mused.

"And you beat the Germans?"

"Of course. 16 to 1."

"So they did score one goal against us? How did that happen, sir?"

"The goalie was blinded by the sun. He dove to the wrong corner."

"Bad luck, eh, sir. But we showed them a thing or two, didn't we?"

"Absolutely. Keep things up and you'll make the fatherland as proud of you as it was of me. Then you'll be a champion, too."

"You bet, sir. That's my plan. Only I have so much homework, and I still don't have my own room."

"You will, sooner or later. And at the rate you're going, one day you'll be as tall as I am."

"How tall are you, sir?"

"About two and a half meters, my boy."

"Wow. And where is your dog?"

"Staying at a friend's. But when I get her back, we'll throw the ball for her again on the beach. Deal?"

"Yessirree! I salute you, and pledge to do my best."

Andrej responded to the salute by bringing two fingers to his bandaged head. The boy turned on his heels and marched off through the group of pelicans, who grudgingly made way for him.

The faded posters in Schmitz's shop window were not much of an advertisement for Agfa film. The door was open, and Andrej had to duck so as not to bang his head. Old Schmitz was reading a newspaper that lay open on the counter.

"Andrej! Dear boy!" he cried. "Let me embrace you!"

"Careful, my shoulder . . . ," Andrej said, averting Schmitz's grip.

"Ach, man, you're so tall I can barely reach your waist," Schmitz laughed and pressed his face against Andrej's chest. "Are you on the mend? You had me scared out of my wits."

"Doing well, don't you worry."

Andrej patted the diminutive old codger on the back and looked benignly down at him. Sometimes he enjoyed his above-average height.

"Did you see it happen?"

"Oh, yes. I was sitting outside the café. When I saw you lying there I thought, 'My son is about to die.' You've always been like a son to me, you know. I was the first to visit you in the hospital, too, remember? Probably not, you were still unconscious and hooked up to all those tubes. Did you like the carnations?"

"Beautiful, thank you," Andrej replied, without the faintest recollection of any flowers. "How's business? By the way, do people ever pay with foreign cash, or just dinars?"

"Well, foreign currency, that's only once in a blue moon. Sometimes a few German marks."

"No British pounds?"

"I've got one in the cash register."

"May I see?"

"Of course. Have a look."

The Queen smiled out from a one-pound note. "Please bring me to Miss Joyce Kimberley at the Hotel Esplanade," she seemed to be saying. Andrej slid it back under the clip.

"I'm not so keen on foreign money," Schmitz said, pointing to the newspaper. "When you see what all is going on in the world . . ."

"Like what?"

"Like Israeli soldiers siccing dogs on Palestinian demonstrators! Just look at this photo. I'm telling you, they should never have been given their own country. As long as there are Jews, there'll be no peace."

"Ohhh," said Andrej, against his better judgement, "I think they deserved a chance. After all, they nearly got wiped out here."

"Nearly, yes. And if we'd had another two years, it would have succeeded, too. And if the world wants to give them a chance, why Palestine, of all places? Why not Madagascar? Hitler even offered it to them!"

"Maybe because they wanted to return to their Holy Land?"

A peeved Schmitz glowered at him through his thick glasses.

"I've explained it to you a hundred times, Andrej. If everyone insisted on returning to where they were before the Great Migration—and that's even more recently than when the Jews left Palestine—"

"—then the world would disintegrate into utter chaos," Andrej interrupted. "I know how you feel about it."

"If those Jew-friends are serious about it, then let them put their money where their mouth is. Instead of stealing land from those poor Arabs they should give up some of their own land. Let the Jews have Florida! There are plenty of them there already, and they've got palm trees there, too."

"Great solution. But listen, about my accident . . . I want to thank everyone who was so quick to help. That was pretty much everybody at Café Rubin, right? But who did what? For instance, who took care of the mail that was still in my bags?"

"Gee, son, I really don't remember. It was so chaotic . . . I offered to deliver the rest of your mail, but you know I've got a bum leg . . . I suppose it was Mario."

"Who?"

"Mario. You know him, don't you? Tudjman's brother-in-law. The one with the villa. The two of them stopped your arterial bleeding. Nobody knew what to do. Neither did I—it was so awful to see you lying there, the tears ran down my cheeks. And it took the ambulance an eternity to arrive. Mario and Tudjman—they saved your life."

"And I'm going to give them a special thanks. But what about after that? I mean, who took my mailbags?"

"Really, son, I just don't know anymore. We all did what we could. Knević, Marković, the waiter . . . Some people, to be honest, were just underfoot. But why don't you just drop by the café on Saturday afternoon? Everyone will be there."

"Will do. And, dear Papa Schmitz . . ."

Andrej bent over the old man, hugged him, and planted a kiss on his bald crown.

"Thank you for the flowers."

Mario was the manager of the local Avis rental car franchise and had built a one-story house up on the hill just to the north of the funicular. Rebar jutted out of the flat rooftop for new concrete that would never come, for he had requested and been granted a subsidy for a two-story house, but as is it sufficed him and his family. There was a large television antenna on the roof, and a plastic swimming pool for the grandchildren on the terrace.

The gravel driveway was flanked by white pillars with eagles, each clasping a blank shield.

Mario drove a full-size Chevrolet Impala, the flagship of the Avis fleet, but it was not parked in the horseshoe bend in front of the house.

Andrej wiped the sweat from his upper lip with the sleeve of his best shirt and walked to the front door, gift in hand. This consisted of six miniature bottles of whisky from the duty-free shop that he had been saving for years, because he did not drink. Quite a stylish gift, in his opinion. He rang the doorbell; inside, an electronic rendition of "Happy Days Are Here Again" echoed, but no one answered.

A uniformed postman came cycling up over the white gravel. He was tall and sat upright, giving Andrej the strange momentary sensation that he was looking at himself. It was the same high, sturdy bicycle he'd once had.

The postman elegantly circled the small horseshoe driveway, got off, and rested the bicycle on its kickstand. It was a young man with glasses, and at second glance a head shorter than himself.

"They're on vacation," the man said.

Holding the envelope between his thumb and middle and ring fingers, he lifted the flap of the letterbox with his index finger and deposited it with a nimble flick of the wrist, just as Andrej himself always did. A seasoned colleague.

He looked at the bandage on Andrej's head and exclaimed, "But . . . I know you! You're Mr. Rubinić!"

Andrej shook the outstretched hand and asked, warily, "You haven't taken over my route, have you?"

"Oh, no, Mr. Rubinić, I'm only filling in until you've recuperated. It's a great honor. I've even just delivered a letter to your house!"

That letter, written in block letters on thin paper, read:

ANDREJ RUBINIĆ. YOUR CRIMES HAVE BEEN DISCOVERED. TO AVOID LEGAL ACTION, PUBLIC DISGRACE, AND DISMISSAL FROM CIVIC SERVICE YOU MUST PLACE THE SUM OF 3000 DINARS ON THE 15TH OF EVERY MONTH, UNTIL FURTHER NOTICE, AT THE LOCATION SPECIFIED BELOW. STICK TO THESE INSTRUCTIONS AND YOU WILL REMAIN A POSTMAN PROVIDED YOU NEVER AGAIN PILFER ANOTHER'S PROPERTY. YOU HAVE ONE CHANCE. TAKE IT, OR THE CONSEQUENCES WILL BE YOUR OWN DOING ENTIRELY. A FRIEND.

Under this was a primitive sketch and directions to what appeared to be a pylon on the uninhabited hills above the town.

Andrej felt sick to his stomach and lay down on his bed. Fate was playing a cruel game with him. Who was it? Mario? That seemed unlikely, as he was on vacation with his family, and the letter had been posted in town the day before.

Of course he could come up with three thousand dinars a month if necessary, and from the looks of it, he had no other choice. If need be, he could always tighten the screws on Tudjman.

He was overcome by a suffocating, impotent fury against the stranger who did this to him. There should be a law protecting people like him, people who acted in Yugoslavia's best interests, who safeguarded moral decency, and who took in defenseless, abused dogs. Andrej resolved that if he ever got his hands on this bum, he would give him a taste of his own medicine.

Andrej slept until the sun rose over the mountain ridge and snuck up, so to speak, on the town from behind. He struggled out of bed, made tea, and opened the window. The chain he had always used to lock up his postal service bicycle hung uselessly on one of the bars. The stench of kitchen garbage from the neighboring Portabello Grill told him that stray cats had torn open the bags.

The steadfast rock formations on the outlying islands were lit up by the early-morning rays of sun, while the town and the bay remained cloaked in the shadows of the night.

That afternoon he went to fetch Laika. He went when Tudjman would be at work, because he did not fancy an encounter with the man he was blackmailing, who had also been so helpful after his accident. He was, of course, well acquainted with the narrow alley where Tudjman lived. The ribbon of blue sky above was crisscrossed with a tangle of wires and clotheslines. Other power lines, some twisted into skeins as thick as a fist, were attached to the walls with large brackets.

It was dead quiet; all the shutters were closed. On one of the highest clotheslines, a pair of dark trousers dangled by the pant legs; it made Andrej think of Il Duce, whom they had strung up upside down after the war. He sympathized with dictators and felt that, no matter what, you must never humiliate great men, certainly not after they were dead.

Tudjman's wife opened the door. She was a small woman, and Andrej automatically crouched a bit and bent forward so he did not come across as such a giant.

"What do you want?" she asked brusquely, her rubber boots planted wide on the flagstone floor.

The grotesque fantasy that she was the madam of a brothel shot through Andrej's mind, that he now had to tell her what his preferences were, and how much he was prepared to pay— although he had never been in a brothel before, and Mrs. Tudjman in no way fit the picture of a loose woman.

"My dog," he said.

"Dog? What dog?"

She looked at him with her unnervingly bright-blue eyes, and Andrej thought that although she wasn't a whore, she was surely a fearsome sight.

"Laika," he said, and as proof he held up the thin leather leash he had brought along.

"You're not from the vice squad?"

Could she be, after all . . . ?

"Because of my husband. He is an animal. No woman is safe around him."

"No, I'm not," he said.

She began shifting from one foot to the other and looked up at him with an enigmatic smile.

"I know who you are. You're the great grenadier."

"I'm the postman."

"Not when you're in uniform. Then you're the dashing soldier all the girls dream of."

She suddenly twisted a quarter turn, making way, and in doing so stomped her rubber boots on the stone tiles and assumed a military posture.

"You may advance!" she cried.

She's out of her mind, Andrej thought as he entered the house. He had little time to take in the surroundings, although he was curious as to the private life of the man he was blackmailing, and at once realized that the hideous antler ceiling lamp, the peasantish chest of drawers, the faded print of the

83

Eiffel Tower belonged to the man who had perhaps saved his life.

"They're in there," she said, shoving aside a plastic laundry basket with her foot and resting her hand on the door handle. "Do you know what my name is?"

"No, Mrs. Tudjman."

"Everyone's forgotten it. No one calls me by my name anymore. It's Ljubica. Just so you know."

His dog was not sitting as a dog is supposed to sit, but on her backside, her hind legs spread wide, her hairless pink underbelly exposed. He saw at once that she had gotten far too fat. Her belly, with its small nipples, was grossly distended.

"Laika!" he cried out buoyantly, because he had so looked forward to this reunion.

She gawked at him in panic and did not budge.

Half an hour later Andrej was still sitting cross-legged on the rug of Tudjman's bedroom, putting together a jigsaw puzzle with Katarina.

Of course he had heard that the daughter was mentally disabled, but he'd expected worse. She slid the puzzle pieces together more deftly than he did. When he entered the room, she had shaken his hand and asked what she should call him.

"Just say Uncle Andrej," he had replied.

While they were playing, he looked furtively around the room. There was a steel file cabinet and a small writing desk, but he couldn't very well go rifling through the drawers with Katarina there. Yet another half hour later he felt it was time to go, for he did not want Tudjman to come home and find him here.

"Laika, here!" he commanded, holding up the leash.

"No, no!" Katarina cried. "We still have to do the foal. First the foal!"

"All right, then," he said, and he put in more effort than previously, so that the pony's tail took shape in no time at all, as did the yellow flower that it held in its mouth.

But when he picked up the leash again, Katarina flung her skinny arms around Laika and asked with a little-girl voice if she couldn't stay until his next visit.

"Who says there will be a next visit?" he asked.

"Me, me!" she exclaimed. "I have another big puzzle. Of Rome!"

When he shook his head and stood up, she held on tightly to Laika, who began whining pitifully. It was hard to tell whom she feared more: the girl or him.

"Just two weeks, Uncle Andrej, a week, a day . . ."

"I'll come get the dog another time, is that okay, Ljubica?" he said as he made his way to the front door by way of the kitchen.

"Yes, yes," she sang back, "as long as you're wearing your uniform next time!"

In the week prior to the national holiday it was, as usual, busier than normal in town; moreover, as the Socialist Federal Republic was celebrating its twenty-fifth anniversary, the funicular enjoyed peak popularity. Young Pioneers from the surrounding villages were already quartered in the youth hostel, the pensions were fully booked with veterans, and Josip's assistant conductor, Ante Dragović, an elderly man with a droopy mustache and oversized ears whose forty-some years as a Party member got him the job, now manned the second car. Ante had no uniform of his own, and wore Josip's spare cap. He was deaf and mute.

Every quarter hour, Josip's and Ante's cars passed midway, but the two men never greeted each other, unlike their passengers, who waved enthusiastically to one another.

These were glorious, clear spring days, and lines even formed at the ticket booth.

Ante's face, aided by the droopy mustache, was as ill humored as always, but Josip, too, looked gruff and stiffly ceremonious; it in no way betrayed the immense pride he felt inside. The passengers might laugh exuberantly, chat among themselves, and point to features of interest—the Turkish fort, the domes of the Saint Anastasia church, an oil tanker—but he stoically held the brake handle and kept his eyes glued to the rails. For the passengers, this was an exciting excursion, but he mustn't let on that packed cars and constant action meant anything special to him. No one could know that outside this festive period he was, sometimes for weeks on end, the only passenger on the trip up the hill to eat his lunch at the heroes' monument, and on the way back down an hour later. And that, at the beginning or the end of each workday, he would have to climb and descend the steep path to fill the upper car with water ballast. Josip was pleased to be observed by so many people in his function as chief operator of the funicular. He opened and closed the doors, decided who could board and who had to wait until the next car; he deftly attached and removed the water hose and reveled in the amazed admiration that the ingenious water ballast technique, introduced more than a century ago, still elicited from the younger riders.

Although his uniform was, strictly speaking, no longer that of a civil servant, he still wore his Order of the People's Army medallion. The older veterans, whom he always gallantly offered the seats with the best view—at the back on the way up, at the front on the way down—were often decorated with medals. He always saluted them while opening or closing the doors, and the ones who were not too old or blind to notice his modest award responded in kind.

These were marvelous days indeed. How he would have liked to invite Jana to see him in his full glory, but he did not dare. She was, for all her delightful qualities, not the kind of woman who could resist publicly flaunting her intimacy with the chief operator; and as a mondaine lady from Zagreb she would naturally stick out in a crowd like this. What if she wore net stockings? He wouldn't put it past her! But he had no objection to Schmitz, who did a roaring trade taking snapshots of the visitors—they paid him in advance and picked up their photos the next day at his shop—offering Josip prints of the shots in which he appeared at his most flattering. He looked forward to sharing these with her.

According to the weather forecast, there was a chance of rain later that afternoon, but to Josip's relief the skies remained clear and the jagged ridge of the mountains contrasted sharply against the immaculate blue. Among the last group—the sun was already low and cast a wide, blindingly glistening streak across the sea—was Mario. Now, more than ever, Josip was relieved he did not invite Jana, for Mario was an incorrigible womanizer and would undoubtedly have pestered her.

In that same party was their former commander, the legendary Colonel Nicola Modrić, under whose command they had fought in the mountain passes above Senj. Schmitz joined them as well, tripod and all, for this VIP visit was begging for a photo at the heroes' monument.

Josip's heart raced when the colonel invited Mario and him for a group photo on the marble steps. Wait till Jana sees this, he thought.

Mario, who was wearing a tailored dark-blue suit but no necktie, borrowed Schmitz's and quickly knotted it.

And there they were: three stiff older men posing before their own monument, all three wearing sunglasses due to the low-lying sun that cast a shadow of the photographer at their feet.

When the car, on its descent, approached the passing tracks, the only thing that bothered Josip was the envelope of money in the inside pocket of his uniform, which he soon had to deposit under that cursed concrete block on the shoulder of the Ulica Zrinskog.

The cars made their customary elegant divergence, each momentarily on its own track. Ante did not wave; nor did Josip.

In the other, ascending, car sat Andrej.

He had intentionally waited until it was Ante's turn to man the upward car and took a window seat on the north side to minimize the chance that Josip would spot him.

In his inside pocket was an envelope of money, which he was, according to the blackmailer's instructions, to deposit at the base of a transmission tower in the hills.

That April afternoon in 1988 marked the beginning of their mutual dependence.

PART 3

Andrej had resumed his work as a postman and had been given a new bicycle. Josip visited Jana every six weeks and took comfort from the thought that his daily climb to the heroes' monument to refill the upper car's water ballast was at least good for something: it kept him in shape for his lover, who, while not so young herself anymore, was still a far sight more youthful than he.

In the first months of that year the political unrest in the country reached a head, not only in Kosovo, where the resistance to Serbian domination grew, but also in Croatia itself; this was exacerbated by the fact that the incoming chairman of the presidium, which was chaired by each federal republic in turn, would now be a Serb.

Both men gradually became less bothered by the blackmail to which they were subjected. They had gotten more or less accustomed to the monthly payments, and they put themselves in the clear by demanding a new amount each month from their respective victim. Thus they unwittingly created, one could say, a kind of circular bookkeeping. It was likewise perfectly normal that the amount they demanded of each other was adjusted for inflation. In a sense it was even reassuring, as though each considered the other a reliable and realistic business partner.

Andrej still frequented the casino in Rijeka, and he made a point of lodging in a three-star hotel, a definite step up from the first time, back when he'd had the photos developed. To be on the safe side, he stopped opening letters, so he was set back financially. All the more so because he had taken up a new, costly hobby: luxury malt whisky. He had drunk those small bottles he had planned on giving to Mario and had acquired such a taste for it that he bought a full bottle of each brand every time he was in Rijeka. All told, the best solution was to keep demanding more money from Tudjman. He did not take any pleasure in this, because, after all, blackmailing Tudjman had never been anything personal, and moreover the man had likely saved his life. It was really the fault of the criminal who was blackmailing *him* for missteps he had made in the past, but no longer committed. Andrej even got written up in the union magazine: he had been named Worker of the Month for having returned to his route so shortly after his accident. It infuriated him that some dirty rat would take advantage of his vulnerability while he lay injured in the hospital.

He never did identify the culprit. When he went to Café Rubin on Saturday afternoon to thank all those Good Samaritans and offer a round of drinks, the accounts of the accident were so garbled, so peppered with self-praise, so contradictory when it came to who did what, that he left no closer to the truth than before. The men were not even all that interested in the details. They had all been his rescuer and helper, naturally with the leading roles for Tudjman—who wasn't even here; Andrej had seen him waiting for the bus to Zagreb—and Mario, who had stopped his arterial bleeding. Now he, who had never been to their local hangout before, had been more or less welcomed into their circle, a club that most likely also included his Judas. They asked his opinion about the soccer league and the Eurovision Song Contest, and he was invited to join them on a regular basis.

An encounter couldn't be put off forever, although they both dreaded it, if only because Laika was still staying at the Tudjmans' and this required making certain arrangements. It happened differently than expected.

Andrej had gone to visit Laika and Katarina, certain that Tudjman would, as usual, be seated in his kiosk. But the heroes' monument and the upper station were cloaked in a thick, low cloud, and as Josip did not expect even a single passenger to show up, he closed early and went home.

His wife was in the kitchen, making an enormous racket with pots and pans. This show of domesticity surprised him, for she did not cook.

Katarina and the postman were seated on the bedroom rug, putting together a jigsaw puzzle. She was wearing his cap, which covered the better part of her face. The dog lay on its back on the bed, baring her sharp teeth.

Andrej looked up, taken aback, as was Josip, who could not find the words for the touching sight of the young bean-pole being so fatherly with his daughter. The idea that he was blackmailing this good-hearted young man cut him to the quick.

Fortunately Katarina leapt up and rescued them from the awkward silence. She performed an enthusiastic dance, holding the oversized cap on her head to keep it from falling off.

"Papa, look what Uncle Andrej and I are doing! Look!"

Grateful for the distraction, he glanced at the puzzle on the rug and blinked, confused.

Nothing about it was right. The hindquarters of a white mare stuck out of the dome of Saint Peter's, and somewhere down at the bottom, a fragmented foal chewed on half a yellow flower. Other bits of the puzzle were just white, because the pieces had been put in face down.

"Pretty, huh? Pretty, huh?" Katarina squealed.

Andrej stood up, straightened his jacket, and, smiling apologetically, said, "Now there's a new one for you: these puzzles come from the same manufacturer, and the pieces are identical, too."

"Ah, that explains it," Josip said.

Andrej pulled himself together and stuck out his hand.

"Mr. Tudjman—may I thank you for taking care of my dog and for saving my life."

"It was nothing, Mr. Rubinić—anyone would have done the same," Josip replied and shook his hand.

In this way the two men, both in uniform, cemented their acquaintance.

"Papa, Papa!" Katarina screeched, hanging on to his pant leg. "Puzzle! Puzzle!"

"I'll just take the dog out," Josip said, and snapped his fingers. Laika slid off the edge of the bed, sluggish as an overfed alligator.

"Would you be able to keep her awhile longer?" Andrej asked.

"Of course," said Josip. "My daughter's crazy about her."

"I'll reimburse you for her food, naturally."

"No problem at all, Mr. Rubinić!" Josip laughed. "We're glad to have Laika stay with us. Take your time with the puzzle. I'll be back in half an hour."

Andrej felt that he weathered the confrontation admirably. And he felt sympathy for Tudjman. The man had a kind of dignity, despite his terrible domestic situation. If he could skip a visit to the casino once in a while, he might be able to give Tudjman a break in the future.

The debates at Café Rubin became more and more heated, although Knević did his best to maintain a degree of impartiality. Most of them agreed that Croatia should become an independent nation. Yugoslavia was dead and gone ever since the demise of the great leader. The controversy regarding the autonomy of the provinces of Kosovo and Vojvodina flared up again, and Marković was in favor of forming militias comprised of men like him. Those who were acquainted with war, such as Mario and Josip, were more restrained. The men grudgingly put up with old Schmitz's anti-Semitic tirades; he tarred the Serbians, Jews, Muslims, and Gypsies with the same brush and insisted that "Ivan the Terrible" Demjanjuk was a martyr. Everyone, Schmitz included, had the right to his own opinion, but the rest of the townsmen were not much bothered by Jews. There were, after all, none left.

Josip's wife had locked herself in the bathroom and refused to open the door.

He rapped on the door with his knuckles. "Open up. I need to use the toilet."

She switched on her blow-dryer.

"Open up! You've been in there for half an hour!"

"I'm making myself beautiful for the great grenadier!" she yelled back.

"Don't be so foolish. Open the door this instant!" But this time his tried-and-true method—using a stern tone of voice—did not work.

"He fancies me! You can't stand that, can you? Now you know what it feels like!"

"How what feels like? I have to use the toilet!"

But first he had to go to the kitchen, because a pungent smell told him that she had once again put a pair of rubber gloves in the oven. He had, for safety reasons, put a modern electric range alongside the old coal furnace, but this was hardly an improvement, because usually all the burners were turned on, and she put everything imaginable, except pots and pans, on them.

Now Katarina banged on the door as well. "Open up, open up, I have to go, too!"

Inside, the blow-dryer was switched to its highest position, and at the same time, the toilet flushed, and she started singing at the top of her lungs, an approximation of the melody from *Carmen*.

"Ljubica!" he shouted, above the din.

"Who is that?" Katarina asked.

"Your mother," he explained.

"But isn't her name just 'Mama'?"

She flushed the toilet again and opened both bathtub faucets as well. The pressure on his bladder increased.

"Damn it!" he bellowed.

"Damn it!" imitated the girl shrilly, and then she broke into fits of laughter.

"I'm going out with the dog," he announced. "Andrej won't be so happy about that, if he drops by!"

"The great grenadier is coming, and he's coming for me!" she shrieked.

"No, for me! For me!" Katarina screeched.

Josip clipped the leash onto Laika's collar and hurried out of the house.

He opted for their "long walk" along the Zrinskog and then back via the boulevard, more or less circumventing the entire old town center. The sky was uniformly gray and the sea as smooth as a paving stone, but it was not chilly, so he hardly needed his jacket. He gradually regained his composure. He would have to learn to live with the fact that his wife was insane. Flare-ups such as these were, fortunately, seldom. Perhaps he could have her committed. It would have to be a decent asylum, where inmates were treated humanely and with compassion. In spite of everything, Josip felt responsible for her. Life, he thought, was unfair: his friend and brother-in-law, Mario, who was born on the very same day and, if you believed in astrology, under the same constellation, had married her sister, a healthy, vivacious woman, and their children and grandchildren were all sane and healthy. He, on the other hand, had Ljubica and Katarina. And little Mirko, who had only lived for six months.

He did not believe in astrology, but Jana did. She had often said he was a typical Cancer and she a typical Pisces, which is what made them such a good match.

Josip strode on; Laika would have to wait to relieve herself until he had done so first.

His city, he felt, was not getting any prettier. Too many construction sites, the same thing year in, year out. And the new buildings were all so utilitarian; they could not hold a candle to those that dated from his father's and grandfather's day.

There was a small bus shelter on the Ulica Zrinskog, not far from that cursed concrete block under which he had placed a small fortune over the past year and a half. The last time was yesterday. He checked to see whether any cars were coming, then stepped behind the bus shelter and urinated. A sensation of great relief washed over him; it was as though emptying his bladder also released him from the last traces of irritation over the bathroom episode. He buttoned up his trousers, waited until Laika had done her business as well, and walked back onto the road.

He saw the postman some thirty meters ahead, standing near the concrete block. He had apparently just propped his bicycle on its kickstand. Just then, Andrej looked up and saw him. But rather than returning Josip's greeting he skittishly crouched beside the rear wheel and began fussing with the valve.

"Flat tire," he called out.

"It's the valve, I think," Josip said, when he reached Andrej. "You can hear the air escaping."

Andrej appeared quite distressed by this innocuous, everyday incident; he had an edgy air about him as he wiped the perspiration from his face.

"Wait a second, your hands are dirty . . . here, take this," Josip said, giving him a tissue. "Man, what a nuisance."

"I've finished my route, at least," Andrej mumbled. "Thank you, Mr. Tudjman."

"You needn't be so formal. After all, you're a family friend."

"All right, thanks, Josip. I guess I'll be going."

"I'll walk you home," Josip said. "We were heading to the boulevard anyway."

Andrej bent over and petted Laika on her head, to which she timidly submitted. Life with one master was already hard enough, but now there were two.

"Everything still all right with the dog? Or shall I take her back?"

"Oh, no, that's not necessary. In fact, I'd rather you not. Katarina is so fond of her."

They set off, Andrej holding the handlebars of the bicycle.

"But I insist on paying for her upkeep. After all, she's still my dog."

"Of course she's still yours, my boy. So, how are you doing?"

As they walked, Andrej seemed to loosen up, but Josip still thought him distant and tense. That was strange, because if either of them had reason to be uneasy, it was him.

They paused at the Agip gas station to admire an uncommonly flashy red Jaguar, a new model they had not seen before—it had foreign license plates, of course—parked outside.

"Amazing machine," Andrej said reverently.

"Costs more than you and I earn in ten years," Josip remarked. "But she's a beaut, that's for sure. Just look at those spoke wheels. All that chrome."

"And those lines . . . have a look at the hood. How many cylinders, do you think?"

"Twelve, I'd say. But I don't really know much about cars. You?"

"I wanted to be a race car driver, once," Andrej laughed. "Like El Chueco or Jackie Stewart. That was my dream. But well, I'd never have fit into a race car."

The owner of the Jaguar, a young man with long hair and mirrored sunglasses, emerged from the Agip shop. He saw them looking, smiled at them, and held up a carton of cigarettes. "Cheap here!" he said in English and got in the car.

They walked on without answering, Josip holding the leash and Andrej pushing his bicycle with the flat tire.

"What a jerk," Josip said as the red Jaguar turned onto the road and passed them.

After it had taken the curve past the Turkish fort, they were quiet again. Then Josip asked, "And then you wanted to be a pro soccer player?"

Andrej looked at him askance, surprised. "How did you know that, Mr. Tudj—er, Josip?"

"I saw you play a few times. I remember thinking: too bad basketball or volleyball isn't popular here, then a tall guy like him would really have something going."

"Yes, I might have. I've missed a lot of chances in life."

"Who hasn't," Josip replied, but then thought to himself, When I was your age, it was wartime and there were no chances out there to miss. The only chance I had was to get a bullet in my head. This guy's a bit of a worrywart. Must be awfully lonely. No girlfriend—he *is* kind of a strange bird. No wonder he spends so much time at my house playing with Katarina. And those magazines he's so keen on, just for the pictures. Maybe he started opening up those letters because he lacked normal social contact. Understandable, in a way. But it doesn't explain why he took the money. There is no excuse for theft.

"Did you do any sports?" Andrej asked. He seemed nervous again, as though he had to brace himself to ask a simple personal question.

"Chess," Josip said.

"That's not a real sport."

"Not really, is it. And besides, I wasn't very good. I could never remember which way to move the rook."

"What's a rook?"

"Exactly: I can't explain it," Josip said.

They both started to laugh halfheartedly.

"And I like to fish. But not much of a sport, either."

"From the pier?"

"Sometimes. But I've got a small boat. With an outboard motor. There are times I need to get out of the house."

"Because of . . . your wife?"

"Andrej, we don't know each other well enough for me to go into all that."

"Sorry, Josip . . ."

"Never mind."

When they reached the Turkish fort, where recently a new Croatian flag had replaced the Yugoslavian one, Laika began to hobble pitifully, and then stopped altogether.

"What's with her, now?" Josip asked, tugging on the leash.

"She does that when she's out of sorts," Andrej said. "Wouldn't you know it: I get stuck with a psychologically disturbed greyhound. Just the thing for me."

"Maybe she's got a thorn in her paw, or a pebble."

They lifted her paws one at a time but found nothing.

"I'll carry her in my mailbag. Laika, come!"

They resumed their walk along a row of dilapidated and abandoned workmen's houses. The wind had picked up; the smooth sea showed signs of swells and brushstrokes of raw silver. Josip pulled the collar of his jacket closer, tucking it up under his chin, the postman tugged his cap farther over his ears, and Laika peered out over the brim of the mailbag, like a tragic, kidnapped princess being led to some dreadful fate. By the time they reached the harbor the wind had intensified, occasionally reaching gale force. The sea bashed the recesses in the quay and spewed fountains of foam into the air. The masts of the boats in the marina swayed wildly back and forth, like mechanical metronomes run amok.

They were suddenly the only ones about. Trash from the Portabello Grill tumbled across the cobblestones.

"It's the Bora," Josip said as Andrej bent over to lock his bicycle to the bars. "Here, give me the leash, I've got to get myself home."

"Why don't you come inside?" Andrej called over his shoulder. "Then we can check she's not got anything stuck in her paw. I've got tweezers."

"Hurry up and open the door, then," said Josip. "This wind is freezing."

The apartment was just as he remembered it from a year earlier. There were even black socks hanging to dry, the same as before.

"Take a seat," Andrej said. "I'll pour us drinks."

Josip sat down on the same chair, at the same Formica-topped kitchen table, where he had taken the fifty-pound note from Andrej's wallet.

"Nice place," he said, just to say something.

"You've been here before, though, haven't you?" Andrej replied. "When I was in the hospital."

"True," Josip said, on his guard, "but that was so long ago. And you weren't my host then. A generous one, too, I see."

"This here is Aberlour," Andrej said, placing two glasses on the table. "A Speyside single malt. I'm curious what you'll think of it."

They toasted and drank. Outside, the Bora surged.

"I hope your boat's tied up properly. And that the cable car survives."

"It's survived everything until now. Even the Germans. So it should be fine. Delicious whisky."

"Fruity, with a faint smoky aftertaste. Matured for sixteen years in sherry casks."

"Sixteen years? Well, well. How'd you get your hands on this?"

Andrej, suddenly cautious, did not want to say he had bought the whisky in Rijeka. It was, after all, from there that he had posted the blackmail letters. "I'm just an aficionado, that's all," he said noncommittally, "and since I've quit high-powered sports, I can indulge myself."

Josip chuckled and raised his glass. "I'm no high-powered athlete, either. I only booze for recreation."

Over the course of the next few hours—it was still light, even in the semi-basement apartment, and they ate the *blitva* Andrej still had in the fridge, checked Laika's paws, and drank in moderation—Andrej began to feel a certain sympathy toward him. Tudjman was so calm, so self-confident in everything he did. And above all, he felt that Tudjman regarded him attentively, took his comments seriously, and appeared to be sincerely interested in a good rapport. He wasn't used to this. He had never known his father but could imagine that he'd been a man just like Josip.

Josip stayed sitting at his kitchen table until long past nine, while the storm raged along the coast.

"This one's Laphroaig," Andrej said, setting a green one-liter bottle on the table. "The most extreme malt. Almost a medicinal, very smoky taste, with a hint of seaweed and—"

"No, my boy," Josip laughed, shaking his head. "I have to get going. Another time. Have you got a blanket or something to wrap Laika in?"

When Andrej opened the door and held tight against the gusts battering the harbor, the sea, at least as far as one could see in the night, had been transformed into a seething maelstrom. At this point no one would be worried about the fishing boats; if they hadn't been tied up properly before the storm, it was too late to do anything about it now.

"Josip," he said, "are you sure you won't wait it out?"

"No, no," Josip replied and headed up the stairs, cradling the swaddled Laika in his arms. "I have to be getting home. As soon as I've reached the first alley, I'll be fine."

Andrej poured himself a glass of Laphroaig, neat, lay down on his bed, and listened to the fury of the elements.

"Have I ever told the story about the Jews and the funicular?" Schmitz asked.

"Many times," said Knević peevishly. But the others out on the café terrace, including Josip, had not heard it before. And of course Josip was interested in anything having to do with funiculars.

Schmitz sipped his liqueur and launched into his tale.

"In 1944, when we loaded the last Jewish rats onto the trains . . ."

"Schmitz," Knević interrupted, "tone it down a little, will you? What happened, happened, but we're not anti-Semites here."

"I've got nothing against anti-Semites," Marković chimed in. He had just finished his shift and ordered his first beer. "I'm not prejudiced."

"The Jews are no trouble at all these days," Mario said. "That's all history. Now, Gypsies, they're a different story. Last week one of our brand-new Peugeot 205s—"

"Shut up, Mario," Josip interrupted. "Schmitz—what was it, then, about the funicular?"

"Gentlemen," Knević said stiffly, getting up, "if you want to listen to this Ustaša folklore, go right ahead. I've got better things to do." And with this, he took his hat and walking stick and marched off.

"And he was there himself, by the way," Schmitz muttered maliciously.

What it boiled down to was that in May 1942, no less than Himmler himself paid a visit to the commanding Wehrmacht general. The funicular was still intact, but the British had bombed the reservoir, cutting off the supply of water ballast. Of course, they could have installed a generator to pump the necessary water up the hill, but the general's deputy, a brilliant young man who, according to Schmitz, would become the president of Austria after the war, came up with a better idea: Why siphon costly fuel away from the German war effort, while hundreds of Jews were waiting to be sent to the camps? No sooner had it been said than the Jews—men, women, and children, but especially men, because after all it was about ballast—were forced to climb to the upper station and were crammed into the waiting car. The other car, waiting empty at the bottom, was decorated with festoons, and the Reichsführer was welcomed with speeches and a brass band. And when his cable car ascended the hill, much faster than usual because the descending car was filled to the brim with Jews, the brilliant young officer pointed, with a certain pride, to the unique counterweight as it passed halfway. The Reichsführer was highly amused, Schmitz related, and he waved genially to the carriage as it passed. He was so delighted, in fact, that the procedure was repeated the following day: the Jews were once again driven up the path—and this did not go gently—and Himmler and his staff were once again brought to the top elegantly and in record time. Schmitz thought this an excellent plan, provided it was executed consistently, for in theory, working them to death would obviate the need to transport them to the camps.

The others listened to his narrative with increasing discomfort: for if Croatia wanted to be recognized as a nation, and even dreamt of future membership in the European Community, where even chickens were protected, then there was no place for this kind of talk. But Schmitz was unstoppable. Of course, he said, the supply of human ballast would eventually run out. And besides, they would have to take into account the weight loss due to exhaustion, which would then require yet more people to make up the ballast. But, he concluded, if they had solved the Jewish problem in this way, then the funicular wouldn't have had to be decommissioned until 1947.

"What an obscene story," said Marković. "Schmitz, that was really tasteless."

"To be honest, Schmitz, I'm not sure I want to be seen with you at the same café anymore," Mario said. "Or were you just joking?"

Schmitz peered over the rim of his aperitif at the others. His eyes glistened.

"What do you say, Tudjman?" he asked. "After all, it's your cable car we're talking about."

"Funicular," Josip corrected him, laying the money for his coffee on the receipt tray and standing up. "Maybe it would be better if you stayed away on Saturdays from now on."

"This is a free country," cried Schmitz. "I'll sit where I want."

"It's not a free country at all," Marković barked back.

Mario added, "I think we're all in agreement, Schmitz. You're not welcome in this company any longer."

"Why don't you give Knević a say?"

"Knević already voted—with his feet," Josip said, taking his uniform jacket from the arm of the chair.

"Kanto, Hornstein, Tchitchek," Schmitz recited in a sing-song voice. Those were the names of the Jewish families who had once lived in the town and its surroundings. Now chairs were scuffed back, and everyone stood up. Old Schmitz, possessed by a perverse need to exacerbate the matter, kept up his taunt. "Goldring, Benaim . . ."

Josip straightened his jacket and prepared to have the last, withering, word. His voice trembled with indignation and was lower and huskier than usual.

"That whole story is clearly the product of your sick imagination, Schmitz. Our funicular has never been used for such purposes. Himmler's car shot up the hill, you say? You have no idea what you're talking about. If my train travels faster than 6.8 kilometers per hour, it automatically activates the emergency brake."

One sunny June day Andrej cycled up the hill to place his extortion money at the foot of the transmission tower. He seldom gave it much thought; it had become a kind of ritual. He felt that he had found his footing lately, and he took more pleasure in life than previously: in his promotion within the postal service, his conversations with Josip, the adoration of Josip's wife. And in Laika, who, now it was summer, he regularly fetched at Tudjman's and took to the beach for a run, to the admiration of passersby. And he had taken up photography again. Now, too, he had brought his camera, because the last time he was here he had spotted a few extraordinary butterflies—fritillaries, he guessed.

The gentle breeze that blew inland from the glistening bay carried with it the briny smell of the sea and made the shredded plastic sheeting that protected the neglected vegetable patches on either side of the road flap. He left the hill and the reservoir behind him and, as usual, fastened his bicycle to the rusty carcass of an abandoned tractor. Before starting the climb, he checked his shoulder bag for his keys, a can of cola, his camera, and the envelope. He had taken the banknotes straight out of the envelope that he had collected the previous day from under the concrete block on the Ulica Zrinskog.

He would need a good half hour to reach the drop-off spot. It was the last and highest mast in this section of the hill-crest and stood in a parched and stony grassland. Impenetrable thornbushes grew between the concrete blocks on which the pylon rested, and in these bushes lay hidden an unassuming round white plastic tub with a lid: a container for sheep's cheese from the island of Pag, ostensibly just loose litter. The sell-by date stamped in vague blue ink reminded Andrej how long all this had been going on.

When he reached the edge of the grassland he stopped and hung the camera around his neck, because it was here that he had seen the butterflies last time. He had loaded a roll of high-resolution color film. As usual, the place was deserted. When he reached the transmission tower, he laid his shoulder bag on the ground and kneeled down.

On the white plastic tub sat an Apollo butterfly, a *Parnassius apollo*, the most beautiful and rare butterfly in all of Croatia, one which was normally only spotted in the national nature reserve.

Andrej gingerly lifted his camera. This was a magnificent specimen. Its wings, with their six red eyespots, quivered in the breeze.

The cheap plastic tub would spoil a calendarworthy photograph, but he snapped a few shots anyway, just to be on the safe side. Once the butterfly flew off there was no telling where it would land.

He did not get another chance: the butterfly flew away when he approached and showed no intention of landing on a photogenic blossom, and Andrej soon lost sight of it.

"Pity about that plastic tub," Schmitz said when they inspected the prints together, "otherwise it would have been perfect for a postcard."

"True," Andrej replied and slid the photos back into the envelope. You couldn't very well sell a postcard of a white plastic lid with the clearly visible sell-by date 02-03-1988.

"You should get yourself a camera with a telephoto lens, so you don't scare them off. And what's more, the butterfly comes out perfectly sharp while the background is blurry. Here, look, I've got one, a Leica. Almost the same name as that cute dog of yours! It's got a focal length of —"

Andrej cut him off with a shake of the head. "Another time, Papa Schmitz. I'm a little short on cash at the moment."

"I can give you a twenty percent discount. Dear boy, I'm so happy you are taking pictures again!"

"No, really, not right now."

"You know what, I'll give you thirty percent off." Schmitz rested his soft, spotted hand on Andrej's. "I look at it as an investment. If you were to make a really good series of that Apollo butterfly . . ."

Irritated with Schmitz's pushiness, Andrej snapped, "You won't be able to sell those cards of yours anywhere except here. Mario won't stock them at the Avis office, and he'll stop the hotel from ordering them. And you can forget Tudjman's kiosk altogether, after that stunt you pulled back at the café."

Old Schmitz gave him a hurt look and sank back down on his stool.

"Ah, so there we are, I'm a pariah in my own city. And why? Because I dare to speak the truth."

"Nonsense. That anti-Semitism of yours is complete drivel."

"What would you know about it? You didn't live through the war. You don't know the repression we Croats had to endure. And by who? By the Jews, the Freemasons, the Serbs. Now Serbia's about to annex Kosovo and Montenegro. We haven't learned anything from history, that's our problem. That is the tragedy of our fatherland. Do you still go to Café Rubin?"

"Sometimes."

"What do they say about me? What does Knević say?"

"Nothing. No one mentions you anymore."

Old Schmitz let his head droop and mumbled, "The silent treatment. Shunned because of my ideals."

Andrej patted him on the shoulder. "Come now, Papa Schmitz, don't make such a drama of it. Plenty of others here ran the Jews out of town, but that's all been forgiven and forgotten. You're the only one foolish enough to keep bringing it up."

When Schmitz looked up, there were tears in his eyes.

"You're the only one I have left, Andrej."

He took a tissue and blew his nose.

"I've often thought: if only you had been there. With the Ustaša, when we had our own Independent State of Croatia. That's where you belonged."

"Me? Why?" It was not often that a conversation revolved around him.

"My dear boy . . . You are the personification of the ideal Croatian man. When I picture you in that uniform, with saber belt and boots . . . and your height . . . Even the SS didn't have men like that. I swear to you, you would have had a magnificent career."

"Career?"

"Of course. You're a pure example of the Dinaric race. Those Serbs belong to the Slavic race, but we're Aryans, just like the Germans."

"And you, then?" Andrej asked, a bit maliciously.

"I realize I'm different from you," Schmitz conceded, as though he were prepared to make allowances as long as his young friend went along with him in the big picture. "I'm Mediterranean-Alpine. But there's a good reason I've got a German name. My family is from Graz."

"So you think I could have made a name for myself during the war?"

"Absolutely," Schmitz said. "But your day will come. Mark my words, it won't be long now."

"Za dom—spremni!" Andrej said as a joke, springing to attention.

"For the homeland—ready!" Schmitz repeated, raising his right hand.

"I have to be getting home, Papa Schmitz," Andrej said, tucking the envelope of unusable butterfly photos into his inside pocket. "I'll have a think about that Leica."

Josip's recent visit to Zagreb had not gone as he had hoped. Jana was out of sorts. Her bed was not decked, as usual, in red satin linens; in fact, it looked as if it hadn't been made up in weeks. Jana was also without makeup, her face swollen and pale. He sat on the sofa next to an old woman, or at least with one who suddenly did not look twenty years younger than him. But Josip was a decent fellow and did not want to give her the impression that he was only there for the sex. They were soul mates, after all, but even then, a man did not gladly sit for two hundred kilometers on a bus only to find something no better than what he already had at home.

Forgive me, Josip, she had said, I'm just not in the mood.

Of course Josip forgave her, and he got up to mix a drink. It came out soon enough: she had money problems. They threatened to evict her, she said, because she was in arrears with the rent. And this was because her best friend Yelena had borrowed money from her and then skipped town with a Bosnian ne'er-do-well; she should have known better, because Yelena was a Taurus with a dreadfully discordant Jupiter . . . but it was too late now. And on top of it, she had lost her job at the nail salon. To cut to the chase: she was in dire straits. Josip sympathized and comforted her. In bed she made a halfhearted attempt to please him, but Josip's mind was elsewhere, as he was trying to come up with a solution.

Sometimes a man needs a certain distance in order to figure things out. Josip got this chance when the bus got stuck underneath the roof of a gas station halfway home. The delay set them back more than an hour, giving him plenty of time to think.

To start with, he could temporarily demand more money from Andrej. As a full-time employee, he had more to lose if his secret ever became public. The extra cash could go to help Jana.

They let the air out of the tires to lower the bus, and when it had been freed and they were able to continue their journey toward the coast, it suddenly hit him.

Schmitz. Of course. It was Schmitz.

Only Schmitz was cultivated and cunning enough to think it all up—and he was a photographer to boot. And what about that dirty taunting of his, with that cooked-up story about the Jews and the funicular? Everything pointed to Schmitz believing he had some sort of power over Josip, and enjoying it, too. The man was a racist; he was a bad egg through and through. Everyone knew that his photo shop hardly broke even, and that he had practically no pension. His gimpy leg did not offer the least alibi, because he had one of those little cars in which he could very well have driven to the Zrinskog and even to Rijeka.

It was Schmitz, Josip was now convinced of it.

But how to unmask him? Josip was not a quick thinker, and it was only a few weeks later that he came up with a solution.

The political situation had become so complicated that every Saturday it took Knević longer to explain it to the others. At present, a Bosnian was chairman of the presidium and therefore also head of state, a position that rotated annually among the member states Slovenia, Macedonia, Croatia, Serbia, Bosnia-Herzegovina, Montenegro, Kosovo, and Vojvodina. The last

Croatian had been Mika Špiljak. But the parliament, Knević said, was a sham anyway. The Republic, which had for so long been held together by Tito's iron fist, would soon crumble, this much was certain. The Serbs claimed that their minorities in Kosovo and even here in Croatia were discriminated against, and they demanded a border revision, which Knević saw as a prelude to the expansion of Greater Serbia. "And what did Špiljak do for our country, anyway?" he said. "He was toothless. Where did he let the Olympic Games take place? In Sarajevo!"

"He should have seen to it that the games were held here, in our mountains," Josip agreed.

"Be realistic, man," Mario said. "There's never enough snow."

"Oh no? Don't you remember that time we couldn't even find our tents?"

"Camping trip?" Marković asked.

"No, World War II," Josip said.

"Nevertheless," Mario said, with that man-of-the-world air that sometimes irked Josip, "the Olympic Committee had chosen Bosnia years earlier, when Tito was still president. That's just the way these things go."

"I personally didn't have any problem with Sarajevo," Marković remarked. "Jure Franko won a medal on the giant slalom."

"He was Slovenian."

"So what? Slovenians are good Yugoslavians. There are hardly any Serbs there. I still consider myself Yugoslavian."

"The giant slalom and politics are two different things, gentlemen," Knević reminded them.

The conversation then turned to the Hungarian minority in Vojvodina, which Josip did not even know existed. His fatherland basically resembled the bizarre jigsaw puzzle that Andrej and Katarina had put together, where although the pieces did actually fit together, they did not form a logical whole.

Some of them saw an armed conflict as inevitable. Croatia would be attacked, especially if a man like Milošević were to rise to power.

But aside from the debates at Café Rubin, not much happened in the town. The Serbian residents, a couple hundred of them, kept out of trouble, and in turn no one bothered them. Everyone was on greeting terms with the priest of their Orthodox church, and people still bought their vegetables from Goran Kostić, whose standard saying was that pumpkins were pumpkins and needed no passport.

People led their lives as always; their fate was decided in far-off places like Belgrade, just as in the days of Venice, Istanbul, Vienna, and Berlin. At times a shadow seemed to fall over the bay and the town; usually it passed as quickly as the shadows the clouds cast on the gray slopes of the Velebit, but sometimes it seemed to the townspeople that the sunshine and sparkling blue sea might be camouflaging some approaching misfortune and inevitable death, and that life would never be the same.

But most people chose not to think about it. Not think about it, and carry on with one's everyday activities, seemed the most sensible thing to do. It was as if they said, "What does it have to do with us? Maybe nothing. And what if it did? There is nothing to be done. Why fret about the rest of the world? They'll let us know if they want something from us, and we'll see how it all turns out." This was the mentality that had allowed them to survive for thousands of years, while the empires of the doges and the sultans and the emperors and the dictators had all bitten the dust. Pumpkins were still pumpkins.

Katarina had fallen down the stairs and had a strange-looking bulge on the outside of her left leg.

"Why didn't you call for the doctor?" Josip asked when he returned home.

His wife shrugged. "She's fine there on the sofa, isn't she? And that dog of yours is keeping her company."

He bent over his daughter and cautiously felt her knee. "Is it bad, sweetie?"

Katarina, engrossed in a Donald Duck comic book, nodded absently. As usual, she seemed insensitive to pain, and barely flinched when he lifted her leg onto his lap and pressed the knee-cap back into place. Mario had screamed bloody murder when Josip did the same to him back in 1945. He wondered if being impervious to pain was a blessing or a curse. Perhaps the former, if one's awareness of the world was as limited as Katarina's. But he would give her some aspirin anyway and wrap a cold compress around her knee, and he went into the bathroom.

His wife's reflection appeared in the bathroom mirror.

"What are you doing there?" she asked suspiciously.

"Taking care of our daughter."

"*Our* daughter? Who says she's mine? You've been an adulterer as long as I've known you."

Josip wrung out the washcloth, turned, and leaned against the washbasin.

"Have you lost your mind, Ljubica? What's become of you?"

She glowered at him and said, slowly and clearly, "You have ruined everything."

He shook his head, as though trying to fend off a swarm of hornets.

"Listen. She is our child. We have to help her."

"And who will help me?"

"I would, if you'd let me. But you won't."

She laughed derisively, playing the role of the betrayed queen. "You help me? Admit it, Tudjman. You'd rather see me dead than alive. But mark my words: I'll outlive you."

Josip considered that this might be his very last chance to speak rationally with her.

"Ljubica . . ."

"What?"

"I once loved you so much."

This seemed to please her somewhat. Not that she believed him, but the fact that he said it.

"Oh, yes. Almost as much as my sister."

Josip looked her straight in the eye for the first time in years. He was even prepared to take her in his arms, if that would help normalize the situation somewhat.

"Listen. She's our child."

"But I'm not simple, like she is."

"Of course you're not. But her knee was dislocated."

His wife nodded and said, "All right, give me those pills."

Josip opened his hand. She took the aspirin from him and popped them in her mouth.

He grabbed her angrily by her shoulders, but this was ill-advised, because as soon as she swallowed them, she grabbed his suspenders and, hanging on them, she whispered, "I am, too, Josip Tudjman. I am completely dislocated."

Andrej and Josip sat side by side on the steps of the heroes' monument and shared bread and salami. Josip told him, for the first time, about his wife and their terrible marriage. Andrej listened in silence, flattered that Josip would confide in him and afraid that any comment he made might interrupt Josip's unbosoming.

Mario and he, Josip said, had fought together in the war and in 1945 they returned home to a hero's welcome. They started dating the sisters Marija and Ljubica.

"Things were different back then," Josip told him. "Young people nowadays can wait until they meet the love of their life. Just like you're doing. But in those days . . ."

Everyone was in a hurry to marry and start a family to make up for the lost years. He could just as well have ended up marrying Marija, and Mario marrying Ljubica.

"How different things could have been. They were lively young women . . . and of course, we were heroes."

Josip spat out the casing from a slice of salami; it was made of plastic nowadays. "You know Marija, right? Mario's wife?"

Not really, said Andrej, but he knew she was a beautiful woman. He thought her bleached-blonde hair was sexy. He considered bleached blondes, like Princess Grace, even more attractive than natural blondes.

That was a matter of taste, Josip said, then continued. "Marija could have been my wife. She danced with me as often as Ljubica danced with Mario. But you know how it goes: women have a way of making their own plans, and before I knew it, she and Mario were standing at the altar together, and Ljubica and me." It had been a double ceremony, two sisters getting married on the same day to two men who had been born on the same day. An occasion that heralded a new, hopeful future, according to the town's then-mayor.

"But you know how it turned out. Mario and his wife had a healthy son. We had Mirko."

"What was the matter with him?" Andrej asked.

Josip explained, and also told him about Katarina and about the steady debilitation, both mentally and physically, of his wife.

"You've got it rough," Andrej said.

"Oh, what the hell," Josip sighed. "Everyone does. So do you."

"True," Andrej said.

They were silent for a while and looked out over the rooftops.

Then Josip asked, slightly awkwardly, "Has my wife . . . how shall I put it . . . ever made advances? Approached you in an improper manner?"

"No," Andrej said, "but I do think she's got some strange ideas in her head."

Josip nodded. "That's for sure. Especially when it concerns me. She's obsessively jealous. She has made my life a living hell."

Andrej said nothing, and opened two beer bottles with a lighter, a trick he had learned from Marković.

"She is convinced I'm a skirt-chaser. And it's been a while since things between us have gone as they should go in a marriage, if you get my drift."

Andrej nodded and set the two bottles between them.

"I might not be so young anymore, but of course a man still has his needs. And I'm not just talking about the physical ones. You need a woman you can share things with, the good as well as the bad."

They reached for their bottles and raised them in agreement. They understood one another completely, without even making eye contact.

Andrej drank and watched as the rabbits below them foraged and, every now and then, hopped over the rails. Maybe they could bring Laika along sometime so she could chase them.

"I know how it is," he said. "I'm alone, too."

"You're still young. You've got your whole life ahead of you."

Andrej hadn't had that feeling in quite some time, but on the other hand, he wasn't in as much trouble as Tudjman.

After a long silence, Josip said, "I'm going to tell you something. In confidence."

"My lips are sealed," Andrej said.

"I've got a lover. She lives in Zagreb. Her name is Jana."

Josip's plan was simple: he would mark a banknote and the day after the next transaction would show up unexpectedly in

Schmitz's photo shop and demand to inspect his cash register and wallet. If he found the marked banknote, then his suspicions would be confirmed and his nightmare over. That would also be the moment when Andrej's penance would end, for he would no longer need his money.

A single banknote, one with the queen of England on it, once sealed Andrej's fate; now, a single banknote could liberate him.

He decided on a thousand-dinar note, a denomination that, coincidentally, both he and his blackmailer appeared to prefer.

And he had made a mental note of exactly where Schmitz's small Fiat was parked. He rarely drove it, and if it was parked elsewhere the day after the handover, this would provide additional evidence.

"What's that?" Katarina asked inquisitively.

"Papa's going to decorate some money," he said. "Do you have a pencil for me?"

She came back with her school pouch and leaned over his shoulder.

"Draw on a mustache, that's fun!" she exclaimed.

The ascetic expression of the celebrated inventor Nikola Tesla indeed looked as though it could use some cheering up.

"Did he have one in real life?"

"Not a red one," Katarina said as she took out a felt-tipped pen.

Josip thought about filling in one of the zeros—mustn't be too conspicuous, of course—when he realized that all the banknotes were numbered. This one was AE 1860991. He needn't mark the notes at all, as long as he remembered or jotted down the identifying number. He was catching on to this game.

"And green hair!" cried the enterprising Katarina as she tugged off the cap of a felt-tipped marker with her teeth. She drooled quite a lot recently, and as he was wearing his uniform jacket, he wiped off her chin with a handkerchief. She let him do this with her usual enjoyment.

"You know what, on second thought . . . maybe we'd better leave it as it is. Money is state property, after all."

AE 1860991.

Andrej was thoroughly vexed, now that Josip had confessed to the affair for which he had been blackmailing him over these past two years.

Josip was too good for this world—or maybe it meant he, Andrej, was too bad for this world.

This had to stop. If he hadn't been in the clutches of a blackmailer himself, it would have ended long ago. Tudjman was saddled with an unbearable and dimwitted wife, he had lost an infant son, and he cared for his mentally disabled daughter, as well as Andrej's dog. It really couldn't go on any longer, even if he never found out who had been blackmailing him, even if he had to continue making payments so as not to lose his job and be exposed as a fraudster. He considered forsaking the casino and the expensive single malt whisky; the doctor had told him he had diabetes and that his liver readings were cause for concern, so it would be the healthy choice, too. If he lived frugally, he could perhaps satisfy the blackmailer without squeezing Josip any longer. Josip had even invited him to go fishing. He had never been asked by other men to join in their activities and he felt honored, even though he did not care for fish or fishing.

His talent for photography might offer the solution. In Schmitz he had found a loyal admirer; he might be a strange bird, but he adored Andrej, and if he were to succeed in producing a unique series of the Apollo butterfly—such a rare specimen that only he had ever seen one outside the national nature reserve—then Schmitz would make postcards of it, maybe even a calendar. After all, he had plenty of opportunities, with his solitary treks up the barren hillside of the Velebit on his way to the transmission tower. He decided to extort one more payment from Tudjman and use that money to buy the camera Schmitz had recommended, and with it the means to free himself from debt.

A week later he picked up the money and took it directly to the photo shop. It was his free day, and his plan was to cycle off straightaway in pursuit of the Apollo butterfly.

"Why don't you take my car, son?" Schmitz asked after he attached the lens to the new Leica. "I don't need it. I hardly ever drive, so there should be enough gas in the tank."

Andrej accepted the offer, even though he didn't have a driver's license. It was a credit to Schmitz that he would trust him with his automobile.

It was the tiniest of cars, and Andrej only just managed to squeeze into the driver's seat. Going up the hill by car was quite a different matter than by bicycle. He was not unimpressed with his driving, as long as he did not need to shift gears too often. He did have to lean forward quite a bit to see the road, and his huge feet sometimes pressed the wrong pedals, making him nearly hit a goat. Wary of damaging the gearbox, he parked the Fiat so that he could drive off again without having to reverse.

He unexpectedly spotted the Apollo butterfly when he turned to check that the borrowed car was still safely parked on the shoulder, and perhaps also to enjoy the feeling of having the keys to that very car in his pocket.

It was as though a small shred of white tissue paper fluttered across the grassland, but there wasn't even a puff of wind; blades of grass and lavender stalks stood perfectly still, the sea lay silently in the distance at the foot of the hills.

The butterfly was a white speck, and at times even less than that; as soon as it paused its flight and folded up its wings it was well-nigh invisible. A tiny daytime star, elusive and ephemeral.

That is my star of Austerlitz, Andrej thought. He had read in a biography of Napoleon that the emperor often saw a star in the sky that was invisible to everyone else. Austerlitz, wherever that was, had been Napoleon's greatest victory. If he could capture this butterfly on film, that would be his own triumph.

He removed the cap from the new lens and went in crouching pursuit of the butterfly. At the next glimpse he would adjust the camera's settings, even if it meant zooming all the way in. But this turned out not to be necessary: the Apollo butterfly fluttered up the hill, straight at him.

Andrej realized this was a once-in-a-lifetime chance, and his heart stood still.

The butterfly landed on the tip of a stem of lavender, like a veteran fashion model, at a distance of no more than eight meters.

In the center of the viewfinder was a small circle, which was divided diagonally in two; when the two halves of the circle were precisely lined up, then the image was in focus.

Andrej turned the lens, and the red spots on the butterfly's wing lined up. He zoomed in even farther until the insect nearly filled the viewfinder and focused once again. He could even see the tongue as it uncoiled to siphon nectar from the flower, the double pair of eyes that seemed to look at him like the eyes of that brazen young woman he had flirted with so long ago on the beach. From this vantage point he had a vague blue sea and the sky as background—perfect. The butterfly stayed put, posed for him, showed off all its wing positions, waited patiently while Andrej experimented with shutter times and f-stops, thirty-six shots long.

An overjoyed Andrej did not mind when the butterfly flew off when he loaded a new roll of film. This was the diva's prerogative. He did not even chase it when it fluttered up the hill and vanished. If all had gone well, he had just taken a unique, breathtaking series of photographs.

He drove back, parked the Fiat on the boulevard not far from Schmitz's shop, with one rear wheel up on the sidewalk, and walked home to celebrate his triumph with a glass of whisky and a bowl of tomato soup.

But he couldn't wait to see the results. Half an hour later he put the film roll in his pocket and walked to the photo shop.

The sign ZATVOREN/GESCHLOSSEN hung on the door, rather crookedly, even though it was far from closing time. The door was not locked.

At first he did not see Schmitz and thought he might have stepped out to buy cigarettes. But then he heard groaning from behind the counter.

Schmitz was sitting on the floor, one elbow resting on the stool next to him, a bloodied handkerchief in his hand. His tie hung askew over his woolen vest and he stared absently into space.

"Papa Schmitz!" Andrej cried. He immediately sprang into action; he had never administered first aid, but whatever Mario and Tudjman could do, he could, too. He went into the back room, wetted a dishrag, and filled a plastic cup with water.

"What happened?" he asked as he wiped Schmitz's face and put the cup to his lips. "Wait, I'll help you up . . ." He lifted the little old man by the armpits and onto the stool. Schmitz continued to stare into space, as though trying to avoid focusing on some gruesome image.

"It's me, Andrej . . ."

Rather at a loss for what to do now, Andrej smoothed the old man's hair with the damp dishrag.

"Shall I call a doctor?"

Schmitz shook his head, as though no doctor in the world could help him.

"He robbed me."

"Who did?"

"He threatened me. And hit me."

"But who?"

"He took all the money from the cash register. And everything I had in my wallet."

Andrej said nothing but went over and locked the shop door. When he came back, Schmitz raised his head and said, "Tudjman. Josip Tudjman."

This made Andrej's head spin. The man who had just been the Good Samaritan—and now this? Andrej took a chair, turned it around and sat down the way he had seen Columbo do it.

"He came in and said, 'Your car's not parked in the same spot as yesterday.' I mean, what was that all about? Then he locked the door and came at me. I thought it might be something political, because of my ideals, but he demanded to see the money in the cash register."

"The money?"

"Yes. He went straight for the tray of thousand-dinar bills, took the only one there and had a close look at it."

"And then?"

"Then he shouted, 'You dirty blackmailer!' and punched me in the face."

"And you?"

"I said, 'What are you talking about, man?' and he said, 'Where'd you get this bill? From under a concrete block on the Zrinskog, I'll bet.' I said no, I got it from a customer. 'What customer, then?' he asks."

Andrej held his breath. Schmitz's eyes had taken on a yearning look, which troubled him and, in a certain way, put him off.

"From a tourist, I said, but he didn't believe me. My boy—I got that bill from you . . . tell me you haven't done anything wrong."

"No, Papa Schmitz, of course not."

The old man nodded, relieved, and placed his small, liver-spotted hand onto Andrej's.

"And then?"

"Then Tudjman took all the money out of the cash drawer and my wallet and said this was the beginning of the repayment. He said something about a nightmare that was finally over. I told him I would report this to the police. He said I shouldn't, because I was a blackmailer. I said I would, because he was a thief. Then he said something about coming to an agreement, to keep the damage from escalating. And then he left."

Andrej knew he had to collect his thoughts, and to stall for time he took the film roll out of his pocket.

"Here. I think they'll be perfect. Why don't you develop and print them right away?" He solemnly placed the film roll on the counter.

"Satisfied with the telephoto lens?" Schmitz asked with a wry smile.

"Oh, yes. Shall we have a look at the prints tomorrow morning? I'd like to go home now, if you don't need me to stay."

"You go on home, son. I'll be fine."

With Andrej's hand already on the door handle, Schmitz said, "Aren't you forgetting something?"

Suspicious, Andrej turned around.

"What is it?"

"My car keys."

Josip could not just go home. This was the first time since the war he had engaged in violence. I was within my rights, he repeated to himself as he marched down the boulevard with the air of someone on a mission, while in fact he really did not want to go or be anywhere. The extortionist had been unmasked, and Josip had taught him a lesson. Some of his money had been recouped. But only a small portion of it. He did not regret punching Schmitz in the face: evil must not be spared simply because it masquerades as a feeble old man. In fact, he had gone easy on him. He could have given the dirty little anti-Semite a real thrashing. The nightmare was over. Not only was he freed from the vampire who had taken advantage of his relationship with Jana for so long, but he could even look forward to repayment, so that Jana might be afforded a bit of the luxury she so desired. But could he really count on it? Schmitz had threatened to report him to the police. And if he did . . .

Josip walked farther along the boulevard, until far beyond the palm trees.

The sun was setting, stray cats climbed out of garbage cans and slinked off. He casually exchanged greetings with the men down on the beach, tying up their boats for the night. He longed to be close to Jana. A gray-striped cat sat on the balustrade; she observed him but apparently did not think it worth running away. Off to the west, a dirty-yellow-orange strip of light hung over the sea. It was warm, still too warm for his liking, and he took off his uniform jacket. Where the streetlamps followed the rise of the paved road, he turned onto the dark, rocky path just above the waterline.

He suddenly started having doubts. The extortion was over, that much was certain, but he would have to cut a deal with Schmitz to keep him from filing a police report, and that troubled him.

The warmish breeze smelled more and more of brine, algae, and garbage as he approached the inlet where a cement wall had once been built for military purposes, and where now the town's sewage was discharged.

He sat himself on a rusty bollard, just to give his walk a sense of purpose. But soon enough he thought: What am I doing here? I have to be getting home. Whatever happens, a man should always be able to go home. Katarina would be in bed by the time he got back, but not his wife, of course. Josip looked morosely at the vague stars that began to appear, like cowards who came to claim their booty once the day's battle was over. The stench in the inlet was overwhelming.

On his way back he was angry and upset, even though the confrontation with Schmitz had taken place three hours ago and he had a pocket full of money. His own violent eruption—punching an old man in the face—seemed to have brought about an inexplicable change in him. Despite everything his wife did to him, he had never, in all the years of their wretched marriage, hit her; this had, he felt, given him some moral superiority, the feeling of being the righteous one. But now he thought, she'd better keep her goddamn bedroom door shut, because if she shows her face and starts in with her bitching, I'll bash her. I'll beat that moronic moon face to a pulp. He needed the world to leave him alone, at least for tonight.

He put his jacket back on and straightened his posture, in case he bumped into someone.

But the boulevard was completely deserted. All he saw were a few parked cars—Schmitz's was still skewed, with one back tire on the curb. Bad for the tires. Useless driver, that Schmitz.

Josip was just about to turn into the steep, narrow alley that led to his house when it happened.

An explosion high up in the mountains—it must have been on the road to Gospić—followed by a sudden, raging fire that lit up the low-hanging clouds. After that, when the flames died down, the sharp rattle of gunshots. Josip stood still and listened. There was nothing more to be seen, Josip knew, but he recognized the pattern of individual gunshots and the barrage of automatic weapons. The machine guns had the last word. He knew this all from long ago, when he had fought the enemy on these very same hills. The shots sounded different from back then, like an old song resung by another artist. But he did know what they meant. The war had reached their town.

After his encounter with Schmitz, Andrej had walked in the opposite direction, following the boulevard to the south. Where the line of streetlamps climbed the hill in the direction of the Turkish fort, he took the unlit road that led down to the old fishing village and then turned into a winding coastal path. He had no desire to go home, for he wouldn't know what to do with himself. The day was nearly over, but it would not leave him in peace. The sunset was drawn-out and stubborn; orange stripes doggedly kept night from falling. And tomorrow would be another day. Life was more confusing than he'd like. He had the Apollo butterfly, but even if those photographs sold well, he would not be rid of Josip Tudjman, who now believed that Schmitz was the blackmailer. Tudjman had threatened him, and if he kept up the pressure, Schmitz might crack and disclose where that banknote came from.

He had resolved never to send Tudjman another blackmail letter, but now he had no choice, for only then would Tudjman realize his mistake.

It would have to be a letter in the same style as the very first ones, like that postcard from the casino in Rijeka: defiant, cynical, a tad frivolous—the style of an opportunistic rake, from someone who did not at all fit Schmitz's profile and was out to bankroll his playboy lifestyle. Maybe he should book a trip to Saint-Tropez or somewhere similar and write him from there. But then again, his absence might be noticed.

Actually, Tudjman should realize that a postcard from Rijeka couldn't possibly have been sent by an elderly invalid like Schmitz, but he was fixated on that one banknote.

Tudjman had no insight into human nature, no life experience.

The explosion on the hillside took Andrej by surprise, and his first reaction was that it must be construction; but the fire that blazed high in the Velebit just as the sun had finally sunk into the sea clearly meant something else. Andrej had never experienced war, except in TV movies, and the ensuing machine-gun fire filled him with awe. Particularly for himself, for now he was a man who could later say: I was there, when the war reached my town.

PART 4

It was not war, but a raid. Until the early morning, the towns-people assumed it was a Serbian atrocity, but it turned out to be something else entirely: in and around the burnt-out vans they found the bodies of Serbian marine recruits on their way home from an electronics course in Rijeka; they had defended themselves with their handguns, but in the end, they had all been killed. The nationalist Croatian slogan *za dom spremni* scrawled on the doors of the charred wrecks left little doubt: this deed had been committed by their own people. It was still terrible, but better than the other way around. It was just a matter of time, people said; if their own boys hadn't struck first, then the Serbs would have.

Marković had been absent at Café Rubin the week before, and this Saturday, too, the other men waited anxiously to see if he would show up. They waited a long time; the sun disappeared behind the clock museum and cast a broad shadow across the square.

He did finally arrive: on his moped, unshaven, and wearing camouflage gear and oversized sunglasses. Knević ordered a fresh round. Marković lingered for a chat with the newspaper vendor before sauntering over to them, helmet in hand.

He looks like an actor in an Italian B movie, Josip thought.

"Have a good weekend?" Mario asked jovially, sliding him a glass.

"Oh, yes," Marković replied, "I've been to visit my daughter. She studies in Dubrovnik, as you all know." He took a sip but set his glass back down immediately, as though his thoughts were elsewhere, and leaned back.

Poseur, Josip thought to himself.

"Economics, isn't it?" Knević asked, smiling. "So you didn't hear anything? About the attack?"

"What attack?" Marković asked absently.

"Come on," Mario said. "We're all friends here."

"Gentlemen," said the pharmacist, "not everything can be discussed publicly. Not yet, anyway. But here's to Franjo Marković, a true Croatian patriot! *Na zdravlje!*"

"Na zdravlje," the other men repeated solemnly.

Josip was the only one who did not raise his glass.

The next time he took Laika walking along the Zrinskog, Josip gave in to an urge: he picked up that cursed concrete block with both hands, lifted it high above his head, and hurled it with a loud grunt down the hillside. It rolled and rolled and bounced off other rocks and stones before—to Josip's satisfaction—coming to rest far below among the rubble and weeds. The nightmare was over.

Except that at his feet waited, utterly unexpectedly, another white envelope.

Despite the garish Las Vegas postcard, he did not believe for a single moment that the bastard had ever been in America, for there was no postage stamp—but one thing was for sure: it could not have come from Schmitz. Josip had scared the daylights out of him and moreover it was simply not his style. Just like the very first letters, now that he thought about it.

He had accused the wrong man.

Josip took the negatives out of the envelope and held them up to the light. He already knew which photos the blackmailer had saved for last: the one with Jana kneeling in front of him, his uniform trousers crumpled around his ankles. *sorry mate put 3000 dinars in a plastic bag and seal it good because i might not get to it right away i don't live here anymore you'll get the last negative when i get the money*. It had been a fatal mistake to seduce her, or let her seduce him—this was a moot point now—during his shift. He was now more afraid of the management of the funicular than of his wife.

He tied up Laika and made his way down the steep hillside to retrieve the concrete block. He had been foolishly presumptuous, he realized as he dragged the block back into place.

Schmitz had indeed used the butterfly photos, and for a full calendar at that, called *The Pride of Croatia*. Each of the twelve months featured one of Andrej's photos. To celebrate, Schmitz had invited Andrej for dinner. Andrej didn't much feel like it but realized he couldn't very well refuse. Schmitz lived in a small apartment on the boulevard that he had inherited from an aunt, not directly above his shop, but a few doors farther down.

He had gone to a lot of trouble: candles, classical music, *čevapčići*; and he wore a white dress shirt and purple woolen vest Andrej had never seen before.

"Take a seat, my boy," Schmitz said as he tied on an apron. "Dinner will be ready soon."

While he was in the kitchen, Andrej had a look around the apartment. Shelves full of books and small display cases of knickknacks. It was as though the old auntie still lived here. As in his own home, there was a vase of flowers on the table. He did not feel entirely comfortable, and the reason gradually occurred to him: if he was still alone when he got old, this is how he could end up.

It irked him that Schmitz hardly sat at the table during the meal, but continually dashed back and forth to the kitchen for food and drinks, and that he kept his apron—pink with light-blue flowers!—on the whole time. The combination of Schmitz's nearly bald head and his thick glasses, which made his eyes bug out like a frightened fish's, unnerved him even more.

"Guess who came to see me," Schmitz said after dinner, his pursed lips blowing over a cup of mocha.

"Tudjman?"

"Right. He brought back that money he'd taken from me."

"And did he apologize?"

"Hardly. He insulted me and called me a disgusting racist who was capable of anything."

"He's very principled," Andrej said earnestly. "And don't forget, he saved my life after that accident. He and Mario. I won't hear a bad word about Josip Tudjman. I respect that man."

"I know you two are more or less friends, my boy. That's your right, even though I have to say he's getting a little doddering. That's why I didn't press charges. But you know, I think *I'm* your very best friend. That is . . . I never mentioned it to anyone."

"Mentioned what?" Andrej asked harshly.

"That banknote in my cash drawer. It came from you. We both know that, right? You bought the camera and the telephoto lens with it."

"Why do you bring it up now?"

"No reason at all, my boy. I would never do anything that wasn't in your best interest."

"What do you want from me, Papa Schmitz?"

"Maybe I'd appreciate it if you visited me more often. Just the two of us, like tonight."

"I'm busy," Andrej replied, as aloofly and blandly as possible.

"I know that," Schmitz said hastily, fidgeting with the knot in his apron string. "You've got your mail route . . . and you're a member of the Serbian union."

"Yugoslavian union," Andrej corrected him.

"You don't really believe that, do you? Belgrade is behind it entirely. You're letting them take advantage of you, Andrej, without even realizing it."

"What am I supposed to do, then?" asked Andrej, who wouldn't mind being told again how dashing he'd look in an Ustaša uniform.

"Great things are happening in our city. In all of Croatia. We're going to throw out that Serbian riffraff once and for all. You know the grocer Kostić?"

"Yes, but I don't really care for vegetables, and especially not pumpkins."

"Have you had enough *čevapčići*, by the way? Shall I fry up a few more? No? Well, tomorrow evening there will be a little gathering, just to let Kostić and his family know they're no longer welcome here. Take this phone number," he said, and jotted it down on a light-green slip of paper.

"I can't tomorrow," Andrej said. "I'm going night fishing with Tudjman."

"Oh, Andrej," Schmitz sighed.

His wife did not object to his plan to go night fishing. Even she would be hard pressed to imagine nymphomaniac mermaids climbing over the edge of his sloop to seduce him, or Sophia Loren pursuing him in a speedboat.

"I'm taking Andrej with me," he said. "We'll be out until morning. Don't wait up."

"With him? With the great grenadier?" she had replied in disbelief. "Doesn't he have anything better to do?"

Andrej had been looking forward to this undertaking for weeks. Tudjman had postponed it several times due to the weather, but recently Andrej had seen plenty of lights from other fishing boats far off the coast. Maybe Tudjman was ruffled by that last blackmail note. He needn't worry, Andrej thought, because he had no intention of collecting the money from under the concrete block. That was behind them now. He regarded Josip Tudjman as a friend, and friends did not do such things to one another. He asked what he should bring with him, what kind of clothes to wear.

"Dress warmly," Tudjman had said. "I'll take care of the rest."

Tudjman's boat was a blue-and-white wooden sloop with an outboard motor. As soon as they left the harbor, he fastened two long poles crosswise, on which hung the large carbide lamps, and readied the fishing rods. Andrej held on tight to the seat he had been assigned, surrounded by coolers and an assortment of fishing tackle.

"So where are we going?" he asked once Tudjman finally took the helm and they left the coast behind them.

"To Pag. That's the best spot. Almost no one knows it."

They passed a few other, apparently less well-informed, night fishermen and began crossing the dark strait that separated them from the island.

"It's about forty minutes," Tudjman said.

The boat kept its course over the still, black water, and now Andrej dared to let go of the plank and look around him.

As the lights on the coast faded, more and more stars appeared; he had never realized there were so many.

"Now we'll head between those rocks," Tudjman said, lowering his speed. "I've got to look sharp here."

"Is it dangerous?" Andrej asked.

"Nah. I know the way."

A short while later he turned off the engine and dropped anchor.

It was as though thousands of new stars, lured out by the sudden stillness, emerged above the pale limestone and the lightless sea; Andrej thought it threatening, as if the firmament was out to crush him. He saw more and more suffocating swarms of stars.

"Beautiful, isn't it?" Tudjman said, and sat down across from him. "Soothing."

"Yes, nice," Andrej replied.

"I'll turn on those lamps soon. Then we have to sit absolutely quiet for a while, while the fish are drawn to the light. The least sound will scare them off."

"Okay," Andrej said.

"We'll fish with two poles each. If you catch anything big, I'll give you a hand. There are some real monsters here."

"All right," Andrej said, trying to block out the thought of monsters.

Tudjman got up and lit the lamps, which hung just above the water's pitch-black surface. Four immense ovals of light now flanked their boat; in these new conditions the heavens seemed to recede, and Andrej felt more at ease.

They extended the rods. Andrej asked what kind of bait they were using.

"Fish," Tudjman said. "Fish are attracted to fish."

But not tonight, apparently, Andrej thought after an hour and a half had passed without a nibble.

"They're not biting," Tudjman said with regret.

Andrej thought that this was perhaps the moment to open up about his troubles, man to man.

"I'm in a real pickle," he began. "Have been for some years now."

Tudjman glanced over his shoulder and raised his chin questioningly before turning his concentration once again to the motionless bobber.

"Someone is blackmailing me."

"Really?" Tudjman asked, after a brief silence. "Have you done anything wrong?"

"No . . . well, yes, once. But that was long ago."

"We all step out of line once in a while," Tudjman said. "But at a certain point you have to let bygones be bygones."

"But that's just it—it's not a bygone," Andrej replied. "The bastard has been harassing me for years, relentlessly. I'm supposed to make a payment almost every month."

"How?" Tudjman swished his rod out of the water to rebait the hook.

"I have to put it under one of the transmission towers up the hill."

"Clever," said Tudjman. "It's completely deserted up there. I know where you mean, to the north of the upper cable car station."

"Yes. Of course he's clever. But he's a bastard all the same."

"Maybe he's desperate for the money."

"So what? He should get a job, then. I've also got a demanding profession."

Delivering the mail, Josip thought to himself, is hardly a demanding profession.

"People can mean well," he said, "but ill, too. And the hard part is that you never know for sure which to expect. You remember I told you about Jana?"

"Of course."

"She's in a fix, too. She has a heart of gold, and people sometimes take advantage of that. So now she's in debt. And heart of gold or not—if she's pushed into a corner she can, how shall I put it, insinuate things."

"Like what?" Andrej asked, after Tudjman had said nothing more for several minutes.

"Like how anxious I must be that my wife not find out about our relationship. That it was clear I would never leave her, mindful of my reputation and our daughter, but that she, Jana, had after all given me the best years of her life, without any benefit to herself. That I had to realize she, as a woman, also had her rights."

"The best years of her life?" Andrej asked. "I thought she wasn't so young anymore."

Tudjman seemed to take offense at this.

"Jana is young and beautiful, on the inside and on the outside," he said, "and I can only hope you find such love one day."

"Yes," Andrej conceded, "I hope so, too."

"You know, if a woman really loves you . . . if you only knew what she does for me. Nothing beats true love."

That may be, Andrej thought, but if you ask me, she's got you by the balls.

Even if the light of the carbide lamps did shine into the depths, all he saw was the bright reflection on the water's surface. And if the underwater beam of light did attract any fish, they sure weren't planning on getting caught. Thinking he might never get another chance at such a confidential exchange with Tudjman, he dared to ask: "And your wife . . . was that true love, too, when you got married?"

Tudjman took his time, and meanwhile put new bait on Andrej's hook.

"Yes and no," he said at last. "I was eager to marry, build a house, start my own family. I think I was in love with her. But you know the saying: the first woman in your life makes a hole in your heart, and all the others slip through it . . . You're only young once."

Then I hope it's not too late for me, Andrej thought. I've never been in love.

"But it could have been another girl," Tudjman continued. "Her sister, for instance. Most times when people do one thing, they could just as well do the other."

"So we just settle for whatever comes along?" Andrej asked.

"That's what it boils down to, I guess," Tudjman said. "Unless you're lucky enough to meet the love of your life, like I did."

Andrej thought he had a nibble, but the moment passed. It was already half past three; in another hour or so the sun would come up. The sky above the Velebit looked a little lighter than it had earlier, but around him it was still pitch-black.

Suddenly he saw them: at first a double, then a triple row of illuminated dots bobbing slowly up and down. Sometimes they shifted positions among themselves.

"Josip," he whispered, "look over there . . . what's that? Is it dangerous?"

It looked as though the bright-yellow lights were about to surround their boat.

Josip did not answer, but shifted to the other end of his seat; and because the boat tilted to one side, the ovals of light shifted toward the mysterious, threatening apparition.

"Pelicans," he said.

There were dozens of them, and they were all observing the boat. With the light now shining on them, they made Andrej think of a tribunal of floating inquisitors. Most had their bill tucked against their chest, the large throat pouch like the jabot on a judge's robe. Others held their head up, so that the throat pouch hung freely and the large mouth, with the sharp hook on the upper bill, shone brightly in the light. They all kept their wings above their back, as if at the ready.

"Horrible creatures," Andrej said.

"What are you talking about," Josip replied, and he returned to his spot, bringing the lamps back to their original position. All they could now see of the birds was the bobbing formation of beady, glowing eyes.

"They're beautiful animals. They often spend nights here in the bay. Do you know what they symbolize in Christianity?"

"No," Andrej said.

"Self-sacrifice and resurrection. In the old days people thought they fed their young with their own blood from their breast. Truth is, the young ones just gorge themselves from the throat pouch . . . but anyway, that's how it became the symbol of blood donors. I know because I was a donor myself."

"Me, too," Andrej said.

"Really? Well, then you're sort of a pelican, too."

"I only did it for the money."

"Yes, that was part of my own motivation, too," Josip admitted. "But it's for a good cause, of course. Without a blood transfusion, you wouldn't have survived that accident."

"Without *you* I wouldn't have survived the accident. Those damn pelicans don't have anything to do with it. I still think they're creepy."

Josip caught a wayward little fish, no bigger than his hand. He removed it from the hook and tossed it back in the water.

"Has Schmitz said anything to you?" he asked, after a brief silence.

"What about?"

"You would know, if he had . . . I did him a bad turn. I accused him of something that in the end he had nothing to do with. It's painful to have to apologize to a bastard like him. Sorry that I say it like that, I know you and he are friends."

"Well, 'friends' . . . ," Andrej said evasively. "He's always looking out for me, that's true. I don't know why."

"No?" Josip asked bitterly. "Okay, then, I'll tell you. For one thing, he's keen to recruit you for Ustaša. And for another, he's keen on *you*."

Andrej said nothing. He felt that Josip's last comment wounded his dignity, somehow.

"So what did you and Schmitz quarrel about?" Andrej asked.

Josip shook his head. "We don't have to discuss everything, my boy."

He says "my boy," just like Schmitz, Andrej thought to himself. Neither of them takes me seriously.

"Of course we don't have to talk," he said, piqued. "Although it's not like we have anything better to do—this fishing isn't what it's cracked up to be."

Josip nodded, stood up, and started packing in the rods.

"You're right there. Sorry to have disappointed you. Let's head back."

The boat sailed eastward over the gray-blue water with two silent men on board. White fog thickened the air, so the town appeared only at the last moment. Andrej helped Josip moor the boat, and they said goodbye without much ceremony.

Josip was struck, as always, by the postman's somewhat grotesque posture as he walked homeward along the quay until fading into the mist. Their outing had not been a success.

Josip could find his way home blindfolded, but even so, such dense fog was disconcerting. Nor could he hear anything: it was as though all the world's sounds had been muted.

When he passed the Serbian Orthodox church, he felt the crunch of broken glass under his shoes. It was colored glass. The stained-glass windows had been smashed.

One block later, he saw that Kostić's shop had been attacked as well. The racks had been demolished, the crates and chests wrecked. The produce lay scattered and squashed across the entire stoop. The pumpkins had been riddled with machine-gun bullets. All the windows had been broken, and upstairs, where the family lived, it looked like there had been a fire: every window had a black halo.

Goran Kostić came outside and distractedly tied on his apron. He bent over and started placing undamaged fruit into a small crate.

"Wait, let me help you," Josip said, setting down his bag.

"Such beautiful fruit," Kostić lamented. "Just look at these oranges. Better than the ones from Spain."

"Let me help you," Josip repeated, lining up a few still-intact crates. "Is your family all right?"

"Yes, yes. They're all huddled in bed together."

"I'm ashamed that this can happen in our country, Kostić. Leave that cauliflower, the oranges are worth more."

While they were busy salvaging whatever they could, a pickup truck approached. In the bed was a group of armed men, including Marković.

"Just carry on, Kostić," Josip whispered. "They won't do anything while I'm here."

"Bad idea, Tudjman!" Marković shouted.

"I thought I knew you," Josip shouted back, "but I had no idea you'd terrorize innocent people."

"Serbs!" Marković screamed. "They've got no business being here."

"You're an idiot," Josip replied, holding a large pumpkin in front of his belly.

"I disagree," another voice said. A door opened and Mario got out.

"You, too, Mario? Have you lost all sense of decency? Does your wife know you're part of this?"

"She does, and she's behind me one hundred percent. Save your decency for better times, Josip. We don't want any Serbs in our town."

"Pumpkins are just pumpkins!" Kostić wailed.

"Shut up," Josip hissed at him, before shouting, "Who else was in on this?"

"I was," said Schmitz, who leaned over to the open door so that Tudjman could see him clearly. He was wearing a white dress shirt and a purple woolen vest.

"And me, Mr. Tudjman," said an indolent voice. The driver of the truck appeared from behind the vehicle. Josip recognized Horvat, the head of the consortium that had bought the funicular from the state. "You'd better go home now."

"No," Josip said, cradling the pumpkin as though it were a child, "I'm doing my civic duty by helping this man."

Josip lost his job. The dismissal letter arrived by registered mail and Andrej stood by while he read it.

"What will you do now?" Andrej asked.

"I don't know," said Josip. "I've still got my pension, but that's nothing much to speak of. I don't know how I'll survive without the funicular. I've done that work for more than twenty years."

Andrej had resolved not to take any more money from Josip and had put off looking under that concrete block on the Zrinskog, but the temptation had been too much for him. And the money was there, wrapped tightly in plastic. At the time it seemed to him a good way to make Tudjman, who until now had avoided taking part in the national struggle, contribute to the cause. But now, seeing the predicament Tudjman was in, he felt guilty about it.

Tudjman bent over and patted Laika on the head.

"Everything will work out, girl," he said.

Andrej folded his hands behind his back. This might be the last time he and Tudjman would stand here in the familiar office of the funicular station.

"There's no one who can take over, either," Tudjman said. "No one who knows the ropes. The funicular is doomed."

"But you'll still be able to make ends meet, won't you?" Andrej asked.

"We'll see," Tudjman replied. "Katarina should really be moved to a different school. 'Special education,' you know. But that's expensive."

"I could lend you money," Andrej blurted out.

"You want to lend me money?"

"Why not? We're friends, aren't we?"

"Yes, we are. But you should think of your own future. Your job at the postal service might come under threat one of these days."

"I doubt it. I'm employed by the Yugoslavian state."

"As long as it still exists."

"No point in refusing, Josip," Andrej said sternly, and started marching back and forth. "You are my friend and it's my duty to help. There's no avoiding it, for either of us."

He had the thick wad of money from under the concrete block in his pants pocket, but his experience with Tudjman and that identified banknote had taught him not to make any rash moves.

"I'll bring you four thousand dinars tomorrow," he said.

"Andrej—I don't know if I'll ever be able to repay it . . ."

"Even if you never do," he insisted, "we are friends."

"Yes," Tudjman sighed, "we're friends." He got up to hug him. "If you only knew how much this means to me. Thank you."

Andrej embraced him, placing his hands on Tudjman's broad back, something he had never done before.

"Everything will work out, you'll see," he whispered.

On his last day of work, Josip ate his sandwich, as usual, on the steps of the heroes' monument, and reflected on his life.

He had not been exactly friendly to Andrej at the end of their fishing outing, and his offer made a real impression on him. One often assumed the best or the worst in someone, and it threw you off when they did the opposite. From Andrej, with his dishonest past and his egotistical lifestyle, he had never expected so much generosity. Whatever happened, he would not demand so much as another dinar from him. That was history. With the four thousand dinars Andrej had lent him he could, despite that last payment to the blackmailer and the loss of his job, make ends meet for a little while longer.

He mused on how it was possible that the men in his life turned out to be so much more reliable than the women and wondered if he himself had something to do with it, but he was at a loss for an answer.

Josip took one last look at the track that lay at his feet, at least his last as its chief operator. If he were ever to return, the funicular might be the same, but he would not. Down in the lower station he would remove his uniform and hang it in the closet for the last time.

A low haze clung to the town, even though the sky itself was blue. Only the clock tower stuck out, the gilded numbers and hands of the clock gleaming in the sunlight. From under the cloud a cacophony of honking cars and blaring megaphones emerged, for there was a demonstration in progress against the declaration of the so-called Independent Serbian Republic of Krajina on Croatian territory. Whatever happens, Josip thought, this is and will always be my city.

He had little appetite, and he packed up what was left of his lunch. He could feed it to the rabbits on the way back down, as a sort of farewell present.

Josip stood up and looked around. His eyes settled on the spot of his and Jana's first rendezvous, and he thought: at least they can't take that away from me. He looked up at the bronze heroes, resolutely placed his cap on his head, and decided not to return it.

Josip got in and released the brakes for the last time. The cable car shifted into motion, and he began his descent into the fog, out of which the other car soon approached. He turned halfway and watched the unmanned car ascend until the haze that separated them obscured it from view.

For the first time in twenty years, he did not have to think about who would refill that car with water ballast.

Andrej was relieved to be able to give the money back to Josip. By adding an extra thousand dinars he had even done a good deed, and he felt he could now drop in on the Tudjmans again. Katarina, however, was no longer so keen on his company. Girls her age were fickle, just like Stéphanie of Monaco, who had once been his dream princess but was now carrying on with her bodyguards. Pop music blared from Katarina's room, and she had no interest whatsoever in jigsaw puzzles. Equally disappointing was that Laika hardly seemed to recognize him anymore. She was, it appeared, oblivious to the fact that he had saved her life, and just lay there when he walked in. Tudjman—who it was all about, in fact—was almost never home. But his wife was, and her behavior became more and more peculiar.

"Tudjman isn't here," she said. "He's elsewhere. He's always elsewhere. Elsewhere is better, he thinks."

And it wasn't just that persistent use of the word "elsewhere," which was out of place in her vocabulary. "Do you know how I wait for him every night, ever since our wedding night? Shall I tell you, great grenadier?"

And before Andrej could cut her off, she continued: "I receive him the way we learned it from our mothers, according to tradition. With my skirt pulled up in the front, the hem tucked behind my belt. In one hand a glass of wine, in the other a plate of olives. And a whip clenched between my teeth. That means: You are my lord and master, I offer you food and drink, take me, beat me, do with me what you will. This is how I have done it every night for the past forty years. But he does not want me. He has a whore in Zagreb, and he prefers to go there."

"I'll stop by again in a few days," Andrej said.

From Katarina's room came the thumping beat of New Kids on the Block. Ljubica stubbed out a cigarette in the ashtray, put a hand on his arm, and whispered confidentially, "You know me as a decent married woman, Andrej. Always caring, always serene. But can you imagine how lonely I am sometimes?"

Serene was likewise a word that he would hardly expect from—or associate with—her, and Andrej wondered where she picked it up. He was anxious to leave.

"See you soon," he said and was relieved she did not try to keep him from going.

They sat at the kitchen table in Andrej's semi-basement apartment. Cellophane-wrapped calendars featuring his butterfly pictures were stacked on the table.

"I've lost my job," Andrej said.

"How come?" Josip asked.

"Because the postal service no longer exists," Andrej replied. "Belgrade has cut us off from the rest of the world."

Croatia had declared independence and was therefore at war with Serbian-dominated Yugoslavia. Dubrovnik, Vukovar, Zadar, Gospić, and many other cities had been attacked; the Croatians, who had no army of their own, only a police force, were unable to offer any resistance. The United Nations remained neutral.

"So what now?"

Andrej shrugged his shoulders. "No idea. Die for the fatherland, maybe?"

"Foolish idea, my boy. The fatherland needs living men, not dead ones. Is there any more tea?"

"I'll make a new pot," Andrej said.

"Listen," Josip said. "We're in the same boat. Both of us without a job. You helped me, now I'll help you. I can lend you some money."

"You lend me money?" Andrej laughed. "Come on. So far you still owe me four thousand dinars."

"I know. But if you get into dire straits . . ."

"Don't be ridiculous, Josip. I want to help you, and don't need help in return. How does your state pension stand, by the way?"

"Haven't received anything in two months," Tudjman conceded.

"That's what I mean. Damn, I'm out of tea bags."

"Reuse that one then," Josip said. "It's almost as good."

The Yugoslavian fleet blocked all the Croatian harbors, including theirs. And while fishery was now more important than ever, no one dared go farther than a few hundred meters off the coast; rumors circulated of private boats being fired at near Karlobag, either as intimidation or simply for target practice. And since everyone recalled the attack on the Serbian marine recruits, it seemed wise to steer clear of the gray monsters that patrolled on the horizon. Low-flying MiGs screeched over the town on their way to Zadar or Dubrovnik. Croatia's own improvised air force consisted of only a few repurposed Antonovs, which in peacetime had been used to fight forest fires.

New fighting units, usually with no more than thirty men each, were formed with fierce-sounding names like the Bulls or the Eagles.

For now, the town was spared, but everyone knew it was only a matter of time before the war reached them. And it would not be an occupation like with the Germans; this enemy was intent on driving them out of their homes for good. The wallflower of history was about to be raped.

Everything changed from one day to the next. Someone who had an income yesterday was unemployed today, consumer goods ran out, there was no more postal delivery, garbage was not picked up, buses stopped running, and the tourists stayed away.

On the other hand, everything stayed as it always was: the sea was still blue, the mountain range unspoiled and unchanging, the palm trees on the boulevard upright and tropical in their concrete planters. The pelicans, too, behaved as they always had, as did the stray cats and, as far as circumstances allowed, the people themselves.

It was the illusion of resilience that convinced the residents of the town that they would weather this one out, too, that their way of life could resist every menace the world might present them. But deep down, everyone was afraid.

If even the Romanesque cathedral of Zadar, a city not even two hours' drive away and where many of the townspeople had family, could be destroyed by Serbian mortar fire, then it was not inconceivable that a bomb might fall on one's own house here.

A strange atmosphere prevailed in the town. When people saw and greeted one another in public, for instance on the boulevard, they involuntarily wondered whether they would ever see the other one again. Such an everyday sight as children playing on the beach likewise raised the thought of whether it might be the last time. The light that summer seemed brighter than ever, as though each ordinary scene was intended to be imprinted in the townspeople's memory. Life as they knew it could cease to exist, but this was hardly ever discussed, because everyone thought they were the only one who felt this way.

"You seem to know how it works," Horvat said.

"Naturally," Andrej replied as he uncoupled the hose from the water reservoir. It went without saying that he had learned how the funicular was operated from Josip Tudjman.

"The cable car will stay operational," Horvat said when Andrej released the brake and the car started its stately descent. "It's not about profits, of course—there's no tourism anymore, after all. It's a matter of national importance."

"What do you mean by that, exactly?" Andrej asked, pulling down his cap a bit more tightly. He would not be given a new uniform, and the one Tudjman had left behind in the base station's closet was of course too small. The cap was the spare one Ante Dragović had always worn as assistant operator, and it was so small that Andrej could hardly get it to stay on his head.

"Strategic considerations," said the lieutenant of the militia, a stout man in an olive-green uniform jacket and black-and-gray camouflage pants. "In the event of the transport of troops and equipment."

"And evacuation, should it be necessary," Horvat added. "So we need a reliable man for this task."

"I am a patriot," Andrej replied and cautiously checked whether the car would brake automatically if the driver did not regulate the speed manually. This was indeed the case. When they reached the middle of the route the cars shuddered slightly as they made way for one another, like two courteous elderly gentlemen on a sidewalk, and sidled slowly past each other at the prescribed pace. The rabbits on either side of the rails looked surprised, perhaps because they had not seen the cars pass in more than a week, and in a rabbit's life, a week is a long time.

"You must be prepared to report at any time of the day or night," the lieutenant said sternly, as though Andrej's apparent pleasure in running the funicular was cause for suspicion.

"Za dom spremni," Andrej said, and tugged the yellow-banded cap, which sat atop his curls like an undersized halo, back down to ear level.

"As far as payment is concerned," Horvat said, "you do understand that we cannot, under the present circumstances, offer you much. But once the war is over, you'll be given a contract and a regular salary. My word of honor."

"I am doing my duty for the fatherland," Andrej said solemnly, and he began to brake in time to lead the car slowly and precisely under the eaves of the lower station, stopping just before it touched the bumpers, just as he had so often seen Tudjman do.

Laika had fallen out of favor with Katarina. It was not clear why, but from one day to the next, she would have nothing more to do with her. Katarina was entirely obsessed with a boy band whose outfits included caps and unbuttoned shirts, and she insisted on emigrating to America—to Orange County, to be exact. Now Josip actually did have the time to care for Laika, but the dog had started to get on his nerves. She was so skittish that she constantly trembled, her eyes bugged out of their sockets, she visibly lost weight, and she'd forgotten she was housebroken.

He suspected that in his absence his wife mistreated her, which would be very much like her, but he could never catch her in the act.

Now that Andrej had betrayed him by taking over his job, Laika had become a kind of specter that he would just as soon banish from his life.

Everything would have been different if Andrej had taken the trouble to broach the subject with him; then, Josip would have given him his blessing. Nothing in life stayed the same forever, and just because he was on the wrong side of history did not mean he should begrudge the fortunate ones their due. He would have supported Andrej with sound advice and technical assistance. He would have given him his cap.

Josip was so offended that he considered renewing the blackmail, although now there might not be any point in doing so. Andrej was, after all, no longer a postman; he had another employer and there was a different set of rules. And if you have lost someone's affection and, on top of it, the power to hurt him, then you were nowhere.

He did not relish trying to talk Andrej into taking his dog back, so he tried Jana by telephone, but this was not a success.

"I'm not a dog person," she said firmly. "And besides, it's wartime. If they attack Zagreb, what am I supposed to do as a single, defenseless woman? How can you even ask me something like this, Josip?"

He apologized and considered taking Laika into the hills and shooting her with his old army revolver.

But after he had counted the remaining cartridges, and Laika started to perk up after a few days, he thought better of it.

He put on her leash and took her to the harbor.

Under the clear blue sky, onto which a few clouds were added as decoration, the town basked in the embrace of the bay, just as stately—if you disregarded the concrete crust of the housing tract just outside town—as on the old color-enhanced postcard he had at home, where the hillside was still wooded, albeit in an implausible shade of green. *Die 'Grande Dame' der Adria*, it said in florid letters underneath.

But the situation was more serious than people said. The fishing boats rocked on a stinking carpet of oil in the harbor. Ropes that drooped from the mooring posts and rings into the water were covered in muck until far above the surface. Nets unlikely ever to be mended were piled up on the quay like rotting, dredged-up cadavers. There were dead pelicans, rigid and black, as though mummified for the afterlife. A pelican chick—already one of nature's ugliest creations imaginable—stood on the dead body of its father or mother, itself black with oil up to its beak, like a child after a costume party gone badly wrong.

The same tidal filth that had covered the ropes and the hulls of the boats in muck had left a broad, filthy stripe along the quay and the stone blocks at the foot of the pier, as if the entire inlet was a discarded frying pan never to be washed again.

Josip regarded the coast as a whole. The black stripe reached as far as the eye could see. His town, once a fine lady clad in white, now had to endure the hem of her skirt being covered in sludge.

Without checking whether Andrej was home or not, he tied Laika to the bars of the basement window. The dog was no longer his problem.

Laika was not too afraid of artillery fire, as long as it was far enough away. She had already lived through so much. She had, however, developed into an extremely pessimistic dog. The girl did not want her anymore, and now she was back to where she had been at first. But she was outside, and it was cold. If she sat, the chill of the paving stones crept into her hindquarters, and if she stood, the wind battered her rib cage. Fortunately she was tied up, so she didn't have to figure out where to go. It was frustrating that she could not get to the paper sacks and cardboard containers from the grillroom that had blown across the waterfront, with their tempting scraps of meat and sausage; the wind swirled them around just out of reach. She licked her lips and coughed a few times, surprised by the hoarse and violent hacks. Out in the bay a ship was on fire, and columns of smoke rose from beyond the housing blocks on the outskirts of town. The blast of gunshots in an unpredictable pattern made her nervous. She was afraid that in all the tumult, her masters had forgotten about her and that no one would ever feed her again. She barked now and again, but no one heard. Maybe better this way, because you never knew who would come. A car crept by, piled high with chairs and other household goods, so that it resembled a moving pyramid of furniture, followed by two boys on a motorbike towing a cart loaded with suitcases and bags, but she did not think these were people she would know. She trotted back and forth, shivering, and choking herself every time the leash pulled too tight.

She was used to waiting, but this was taking an awfully long time. A few pelicans waddled onto the square and tried to snatch the swirling cardboard food containers, without success. They looked strange, too, more black than pink, and they appeared to move more uncomfortably than usual, even though they were not tied to a leash. One even kept falling over, and had trouble getting back up; one wing flopped anemically to the side, even though these creatures had two of them. Laika, a thoroughbred racing dog, observed the pathetic action with contempt. It stank of oil everywhere, which masked all other smells. The one pelican ended up just lying there, and its fellow animals abandoned their efforts to find food among the whirling litter. They stood almost stationary, occasionally lifting and then lowering a pitch-black foot, or they turned their heads, which in some cases were still pink, and looked surprised at the sight of their sticky plumage.

Things were not good.

Fortunately the tall one came along, the one who belonged to this house. She did not know if he would be happy to see her, but she wagged her tail just to be on the safe side. He said something she didn't understand, but it did not sound friendly. He opened the front door and went inside without taking her in with him.

Andrej realized he had made a mistake. It was a stupid detail, really, certainly now that the country was at war, but he should have talked to Tudjman before taking over his job. Everybody made mistakes. He felt that on important matters he did make wise decisions: he was dutiful to the fatherland; he would participate the next day in shooting practice with the militia; he had, on the people's behalf, assumed responsibility for the strategically vital funicular; and he had lent his friend Josip Tudjman money. And earlier, too, he had given up his beloved greyhound for the benefit of Tudjman's mentally disabled daughter.

This reminded him that Laika was still tied up outside. He slid the flowered curtain aside and opened the window.

The stench of oil wafted inside, and just at that moment, the rumble of a distant explosion along the coast rolled in. Laika stuck her snout through the bars and gave him a pleading look, her eyes bugged out as though she feared some terrible misunderstanding.

"Relax," he said, "I won't leave you there forever."

He wondered if it was better to have the window open or closed. Open, he decided, figuring that explosions caused shock waves, and the Serbs were unlikely to use nerve gas.

He decided to be magnanimous. Tudjman was a has-been, after all, and had been pushed to the sidelines while he himself might very well be poised to become a war hero. Old Schmitz thought so, too. Maybe as a sharpshooter, if he proved to have some aptitude for it tomorrow.

It was all about some archaic convention, like asking a girl's father for her hand in marriage. Andrej had ruffled Tudjman's feathers by taking over the funicular without first asking his permission. He would do so now, and even offer his apologies. He brought the dog inside, put on his coat, and left.

Tudjman's wife answered the door and said that her husband, who was a monster and had abandoned his wife and daughter just as the Serbs were on their way to ravish them, had just gone out. Probably off to his floozie. Andrej offered a hurried apology and headed for the bus station. It was exciting to walk through the familiar streets and alleys now that they might become a battleground, for the enemy's advance seemed unstoppable. Word had it that Dubrovnik had been destroyed, Vukovar surrounded, and that the United Nations had sided with the Serbs by calling for an arms embargo. Goran Kostić, the grocer, had fled with his family, as did the Orthodox priest. The church had been repurposed as an improvised recruiting station, with a large white banner bearing the slogan *za dom spremni* outside. As he passed it, Andrej glanced condescendingly at the young men waiting in line to volunteer; he, after all, had enlisted long before them. He had shown his true colors early on, and after the war he was sure to be decorated for it.

Marković swerved up on the green Schwalbe he had once bought for his daughter; it looked absurdly small now, with this burly man dressed in army fatigues on it. A heavy machine gun was slung over his shoulder, and his face was painted with black combat stripes.

"What are you doing here?" he yelled, still sitting on the moped, which angrily spat out puffs of exhaust. "Tomorrow—target practice. I'll be your instructor. Take no risks! Go home!"

"I'm looking for Tudjman," Andrej said. "I'm headed for the bus station."

"There are no more buses, man!" Marković shouted. "This is war! Await orders!"

Andrej saluted in a way he thought was appropriate, but he did not go home; he went back to Tudjman's house to leave a message for him.

Katarina looked eccentric in her short white dress and ludicrously high platform shoes. Moreover, she was wearing makeup and there were spangles on her face and arms. She flailed wildly to ear-splitting pop music Andrej had never heard before. The whole scene made a strange impression on him indeed.

"Katarina," he shouted, "what happened with Laika?"

"Who cares," she shouted back in English, and began making bizarre gestures as she danced, including sticking her tongue way out of her mouth.

"Haven't you got anything better to do?"

"I hate the war," she shouted, and screeched atonally along with the music: *"I think you're a superstar . . ."*

Andrej grabbed her by the wrist and pulled her toward him. She pressed her pelvis against him and dangled her head backward. It was the first time a female had ever come so close to him, and it unnerved him.

"Do you want me, do you want me?" Katarina crooned.

"Stop it," he said sternly, pushing her away.

"Oh, you're so ugly," Katarina sang as she flung her hair wildly about.

"I need a pen and paper," Andrej said. "Where can I find them?"

"In Papa's desk," she answered in the brief interval before the next booming number began.

He sat down at the small writing table in Tudjman's room and opened the drawers in search of writing paper and a pen. In the left-hand drawer he found an assortment of office items: paper clips, postage stamps, thumbtacks, pencil stubs, foreign coins, and keys. They were neatly sorted in small round plastic boxes, giving the collection the orderly look of a laboratory or pharmacy. The coins—German groschen, French francs, and Dutch dubbeltjes— were probably tips from the cable car that Tudjman was unable to exchange. Tudjman apparently had a taste for sheep's cheese from the island of Pag, as the containers were all of this sort. He took a pencil stub and began writing on the back of an electricity bill:

> *Dear Josip. I'm sorry if I insulted you. I did not mean to. We live in fast-paced times, and I had to accept the job immediately. Of course I wanted to bring it up with you first, I know how much the job meant to you. I hope that you . . .*

Realizing that what he wanted to write would not fit on the back of the bill, Andrej opened the right-hand drawer in search of a sheet of paper.

Mostly what he found were more bills. He slid them aside and felt deeper in the drawer.

There were some empty, postmarked envelopes, and at first he thought Tudjman saved them for the foreign postage stamps, but suddenly his big, searching hand froze in midair.

It was the envelope that had betrayed him. His hand descended upon the spread-out papers like a woebegone animal that sinks to the ground to die, but then wills itself to move again.

Using his middle finger, he slid the envelope out from under the others. Airmail, addressed to Joyce Kimberley, c/o Hotel Esplanade.

In the next room, Katarina cranked up the volume even louder and screamed ecstatically along with the lyrics *"I need you."*

It was Tudjman. Josip Tudjman, his only friend, had been blackmailing him all these years.

Josip went to Mario's place. Andrej's betrayal had cut him to the quick, and now he wanted to know how things stood between him and his brother-in-law: Mario, his comrade-in-arms in World War II; Mario, who was born on the same day as him, whose house he had helped build, and who was married to his wife's sister; someone with whom for years he had daily or at least weekly contact, and with whom, since the ransacking of the Serbian grocer's, he had not exchanged a single word.

Just as he reached the driveway the big Chevrolet Impala pulled out, loaded, it appeared, to the brim. It looked as though the entire family was in the car. Josip waited next to the right-hand eagle, correctly assuming that Mario's son would be at the wheel and Mario himself in the passenger seat. The car stopped; he bent over and saw only the backs of heads and averted profiles, except for the inquisitive little faces of the youngest children, who still had no concept of right and wrong.

Mario lowered the tinted-glass window and looked at him.

"Josip," he said.

"Mario."

"We're taking the women and children to a safe place," Mario said. "I suggest you do the same with Ljubica and Katarina. My son and I will come back tomorrow. I'm too old for active duty, but I'll help train the younger recruits. And what about you? What are you doing?"

"I'm here to congratulate you," Josip replied. "Today's our birthday."

They had celebrated their mutual birthday together dozens of times—as young men in uniform, as newlyweds with their wives, and many times thereafter; often at Mario's home, but at Josip's, too, at first, or in a small restaurant on the harbor that had since gone out of business. Josip recalled one such celebration in particular back in the sixties, when they stood, arms draped over the other's shoulders, and watched as Ljubica, still pretty and gay, and her sister Marija danced for them. They both wore high heels and polka-dotted sundresses that they hitched up to show off their legs in seamed stockings, and the evening sun poked through the grapevine on the trellis, and he and Mario knew without having to say it out loud that they were the two luckiest men in all of Croatia. And later, there were the big family parties, where Mirko, and later,

Katarina and Mario's children, sat on their mothers' laps. They had celebrated together every year. Recently, though, since his wife had become such a crackpot that even Marija could not deal with her, they usually did so on their own, on the terrace outside Café Rubin.

"Today's our birthday," Josip repeated.

Mario turned away. "I know. Best wishes, Josip." The window slid up, and the Chevrolet pulled out of the driveway.

Andrej plotted his revenge. He removed the photographs from the cupboard and spread them out on the Formica-topped kitchen table. All of them, including the very first one he had taken of Josip's reply to the personal ad. They were dated, so Ljubica could see how long that caring husband of hers had been cheating on her. Of course, Katarina too would be hurt when the truth came out, he was aware of this, but that was collateral damage, and it paled in comparison to the catastrophe he would unleash on Tudjman, the man who had made his life a living hell. The fact that he had learned to live with it did not lessen the heinous injustice. He would destroy Tudjman. He even went so far as to circle the most incriminating details with a red pen: the visible garters on the legs of the woman Josip Tudjman had always boasted about but had never introduced him to, and the uniform trousers around Tudjman's ankles. Andrej would show no mercy. Where had his goodness gotten him? He had been cheated and wronged; Tudjman had betrayed his trust. And to think that in all his benevolence he had even lent the man money. He licked the envelope with the tongue of a Stalin. Even if Tudjman's wife was too stupid to read, the pictures said it all. He even imagined that Tudjman might hang himself.

Laika began whimpering nervously when he prepared to leave, and he gave her a few hard smacks.

"Quiet, you!" he snarled. "You don't know how important this is. You don't know anything at all, you stupid bitch!"

Just then, the face of a young Pioneer with a blue cap appeared between the bars of the window.

"Mr. Rubinić, Mr. Rubinić!" the boy shouted breathlessly.

"What do you want?" Andrej growled as he knotted the drawstring of his jogging pants.

"They said for you to come right away, for target practice."

"Oh, yes, I'm coming," he said. "Mirko, isn't it? Say, you can do something for the fatherland, too, my boy. Are you willing?"

The lad, his blue eyes radiant, delivered the familiar slogan.

"Take this letter and give it to the wife of Josip Tudjman. Make sure no one sees you. It's top secret."

Target practice was held on the field at the dog racetrack, where Andrej had not been in years. The young men had to make do with just one AK-74, the Kalashnikov belonging to Marković. The weapon had a folding buttstock and a thirty-round magazine. They took turns practicing its assembly and loading, adjusting the fire selector for automatic and semi-automatic, and the use of the sight. Andrej was jittery, all the more so because he had to go first.

There was a stack of sandbags on which to rest the assault rifle, and bales of hay representing the Serbian enemy placed at various distances.

"Vertical, vane, Milošević," Andrej repeated to himself as he stretched out on the ground, knees and elbows spread for greater stability, as their instructor had demonstrated, and peered through the sight.

"Breathe calmly! Short bursts of fire! Keep the butt tighter against your shoulder, man, otherwise that thing'll go jumping all over the place! And wipe that grin off your face—this is war, not an arcade game!"

Andrej would have preferred to first see how the others managed, but he had no choice. He squeezed his left eye closed and curled his finger around the trigger.

It can't be so bad, he thought, but he wished he knew beforehand what it was like to fire an assault rifle. He dreaded it as much as an electric fence, especially the moment just before you had to touch it.

"Fire!" Marković commanded.

But something else happened. In the middle of the oval racetrack the earth's crust erupted and rose to an unlikely height, a grubby fist that flung the bales of hay every which way. Andrej opened both eyes wide and saw flashes on the hills to the south. A second explosion demolished the salt ponds a hundred meters away.

"Heavy artillery, damn it all," Marković shouted. "They've broken through." More explosions followed at short intervals, each blast slightly farther away, which was on the one hand reassuring, but on the other hand not, because it meant they were approaching the town center.

Marković took back his rifle and started giving orders. "Rubinić—take my Schwalbe and get to the cable car as fast as you can. They might be evacuating the town. The rest of you—to the rendezvous. No time to practice on the bales. This is the moment of truth. Fall in, march!"

Andrej got up and ran over to the moped, while the others hurried back into town by bicycle or on foot. He turned and saw Marković take extra ammunition from an olive-green canister and put it in his camouflage jacket pockets.

"I don't know how to start it!" he shouted.

"Turn the key, pedal down, easy on the gas!" Marković yelled before heading onto the open field, the Kalashnikov at his hip.

He was probably a hero.

The siege lasted barely a week, let alone weeks on end, as had been the case with the larger cities in the south. The town had been reduced to smoldering ruins in a single day. The townspeople were dumbstruck: it was as though their thousand-year history had been erased in a few hours, like a hurriedly turned page in a second-rate book. This was winner takes all, and to the very end, those who tried to escape the inferno seemed oblivious to the fact that this was not a war between men, but annihilation. The archducal palace was in ruins, the tower of the celebrated clock museum had collapsed onto the square. The hillside housing tract, built in Tito's heyday, was a patchwork of blazes. They had used bulldozers to shove the concrete blocks, which for years had lined the Ulica Zrinskog, onto the asphalt as roadblocks against the approaching enemy. Volunteers attempting to paint a large red cross on the flat roof of the hospital were swept off it by low-flying fighter jets as though they were no more than wisps of lint. The palm trees still stoically flanked the boulevard, but the houses across the road now resembled a row of smashed teeth.

There was almost no way out: the coastal road to the north was being bombarded from the sea, and the exodus was blocked by their own military convoys. The only escape route left was inland, over the mountains. And so they headed up the hills, along the countless paths and dirt roads. Many were directed to the funicular—that ostensibly superfluous relic from the days of emperors and archbishops—to flee their burning city.

Andrej wielded the hook used to pry open the lids to the water reservoir to keep the human stream in check. The elderly and the infirm had priority; the rest had to take the zigzagging path up the hill. He made an exception only for families with more than two children, for people he knew personally, and armed men from the civil militia. This was his hour of glory, and it was as though he had been preparing for it all along, ever since he'd started opening letters to separate the good from the bad.

"Back up!" he warned, pointing with the hook. "You lot can go, you others can't. The car is nearly full. Get in, Mr. Schmitz!"

But old Schmitz refused. "Give me that hook, boy, and get the car up the hill. I'll take over for you here."

"You, then," he said to a pregnant woman. He got in, released the brakes, and the overcrowded car began its slow ascent. Every so often Andrej took his hands from the controls to press down his too-small cap. There were things going on in the blue-gray sky that he couldn't put his finger on, like fleeting strips of light and clusters of small gray clouds that appeared and then vanished.

The hill crept by slower than ever, and the heroes' monument seemed to hide obstinately behind its crest. The wheels slipped and at the passing loop he was afraid for a moment that the car would grind to a halt when they met friction at the switch. Had he overloaded the car? That wouldn't have happened to that bastard Josip Tudjman.

He did not see any rabbits, and the crowd behind him in the car grumbled and groused and vexed him with demands of whether there was further transportation at the top—how should he know?—instead of being ashamed for subjecting the old cable car to such a heavy burden.

He looked back and saw a man with the same cap as his fight his way up the path through the procession of evacuees. It was Tudjman, apparently planning to assist because he knew two men were needed to keep the cars running continuously.

Andrej reckoned he would reach the top much sooner than Tudjman and would have enough time to refill the water tanks and start the descent so as not to meet him face-to-face. Tudjman, with that cap he had no business wearing anymore. If he had turned it in, then Andrej, as the official operator of the funicular, would have had a more dignified headpiece.

He followed the cap, which came nearer with every twist in the path. This was his moment of glory, he was the savior of his people, and Tudjman was the last thing he needed right now. This man, who had once felt like a father to him but was now history—he would have nothing more to do with him. What's more, when he reached the lower station, he would refuse to let Ljubica and Katarina, whom he had spotted waiting in line, board. If they wanted to survive, they would have to take the path. Just like Marshal Tito, he had cut every sentimental link with the past. Schmitz would not give them a break, either, he knew that for sure; Schmitz had every reason to hate Tudjman, and he was moreover of the opinion that the weak should be eliminated. He could count on Papa Schmitz.

At that moment, a barrage of mortar shells hit the hillside, as though an orchard of gray trees was being instantly planted. The car reached the platform, and Andrej engaged the brakes. While the passengers crowded their way up the steps of the monument, he connected the hose and began filling the tank. The water gurgled and sputtered, and this meant survival for countless fellow citizens. He would not seek refuge himself, he would write history.

Just as Josip reached the final steep stretch, Andrej set the car back in motion. Its descent was very slow, meaning too many people were probably crammed into the other car. But this did not matter as long as the cable cars were kept in motion. With his feet spread, Andrej stood at his post, alone, and made the occasional encouraging gesture to the masses climbing up the path. Most either did not respond or shook their fist at him, angry that they had not been allowed on. This did not faze him; he was above it. And who in their right mind dragged a baby carriage—or even, as he had also seen, a television—when running for their life. As he descended toward the burning city and mortar blasts created pillars of dust to his left and his right,

Andrej felt as calm and cool as a bomber in an American war movie flying through the salvos straight at his target. He was too young to have any notion of death, unlike Josip, who leaned, exhausted from the climb, his heart pounding, against the bronze boot of a hero, where for decades he had eaten his lunch. Josip watched the town, his town, burn and knew it would never recover, at least not during his lifetime. He gasped for breath, and panicking that he might have a heart attack, he tore open his shirt, making the buttons pop. Dying now wouldn't do—he needed to refill the ballast in the next car when it got to the top. Sweat streamed down his body, even his trousers and underwear were wet. He hoisted himself back up. In the distance he saw the exodus branch out over the paths along the reservoir, heading for safety inland, and to the road that might take them to Bosnia. The view was much improved, because a couple of the bronze heroes had been blown off the pedestal.

Andrej had taken out his camera and focused the telephoto lens on the approaching car. It was still quite a ways off, but he could see that it was filled to overflowing: heads, shoulders, and arms stuck out of the lowered windows, people were perched on the running boards or hung on to the outer handrails, and some were even lying or sitting on the roof. It was like a piece of fruit being attacked by a swarm of insects. His photos would document his role in the evacuation.

But that came differently than expected. The arc of a Serbian projectile and the path of the descending car intersected at the moment that he depressed the shutter button.

Josip saw the explosion, and how the cars came to a standstill, just short of halfway; and how they slowly retreated while the ballast from the sprung water tank cascaded down the hill over the rail ties. Even from this distance he could hear the fading shouts and cries of the passengers as they were transported back to the lower station. The other car approached, but he did not see Andrej at the control panel. Through the gaping holes of the window frames he only saw what was beyond it: grassland and smoke.

Josip ran across the platform, yanked open the door of the moving car, and climbed in to prevent it from slamming against the bumpers, but he was too late.

Andrej's body slid across the wood-slat floor and under the front bench.

Josip crouched, grasped Andrej's ankles, and pulled him carefully out from under it.

It did not look good. Andrej's chest was blown completely open. His eyes were half-shut and he was conscious, but Josip knew that, unlike with the collision at the bus stop, this time there was no hope. He sat down on the floor and lifted Andrej's head and shoulders slightly.

"Stay calm," he said. "I'll get you across the mountains, to a good hospital."

They started moving again, almost imperceptibly. He looked up and just saw the eaves of the roof as they disappeared from sight. The passengers down in the lower station had disembarked, naturally, and his weight, together with Andrej's, was just enough to set them in motion. Their car descended back toward the town; hesitantly, though, and it would not take much for it to stop again. But Josip did nothing; he stayed on the wooden floor with Andrej in his arms.

Andrej opened his lips, accompanied by a strange smacking sound, like a kiss.

"You okay?" Josip asked.

He could not understand the answer.

"What did you say?"

"I'm all right," Andrej whispered.

"Hang on, lad. Only the good die young."

Groping its way along like an invalid, their car turned onto the passing loop as the ascending car approached. Through their shattered windows, Josip saw shattered windows pass.

"Are they in there?" Andrej asked.

"Who?"

"Ljubica and Katarina."

"I hope so, but I can't see for sure."

Andrej grimaced. It was not clear if it was an expression of pain or mirth.

"I . . . did . . . my best," he managed to say.

"I know you did. Calm now, we're almost there. Pain?"

"No, thank you, I have . . . ha ha . . . enough already."

Was it courage or delirium that made him crack a joke? Josip could see from the treetops that they were approaching the base station. They were going so slowly that it was as if they were floating. He wanted time, more time. He had no idea what to do with Andrej once they reached the bottom. When he took his hands out from under Andrej's armpits, he saw they were red with blood. He looked up and tried to fix his gaze on something, but could find nothing better than the slivers of glass sticking out of the varnished window frames. Suddenly he had the sensation that *his* life was slipping away, not Andrej's.

The car came to a halt. The other car must have either derailed or got stuck.

Josip carefully freed himself and stood up. He peered through a window down the hill. This was not a good place to get out, as the incline under the running board was narrow and steep.

"Andrej," he said, in a businesslike tone, "we have to leave the car. I'll carry you out. Do you think you can manage?"

Andrej drew a deep breath and mumbled something; a new crater of blood welled up.

"What's that? Heaven? No, not by a long shot. In fact, we were on our way down. I'm going to open a door and lift you out."

But when he had placed Andrej at the threshold of the door and climbed out onto the gravel, the floor ledge reached his chin. It was far too high.

"I'll go get help," he said. "Don't you want to lie down in the meantime?"

But Andrej made no move to do so. He remained seated, his large hands on either side of his thighs, his enormous feet dangling out of the car, and stared in amazement at the ruined, smoldering town. He was as grotesquely red as a clown.

Josip laid a hand on a shoe.

"Listen."

Andrej now looked at him like a contrary child whose parents demanded he look away from the television to answer a question.

"I have something to confess to you. Do you hear me?"

Andrej felt fine; despite the joke he had made, he had no pain, only a numb sensation, and he heard the occasional something, and what he saw was perhaps not quite what it was supposed to be, as though he were drunk. And looking at the thick stream of blood running down his trousers he thought that if a person had to run dry, it was good that it came from the chest. He wondered what Josip's face was doing down there.

"I wish to confess," Tudjman said.

Andrej did not understand everything but felt it was only polite to show interest when someone paid you a sickbed visit.

He still regretted not remembering the flowers that old Schmitz had brought for him.

"Speak," he said solemnly. Maybe he could become pope; that was even better than midfielder or war hero.

Tudjman said he was sorry for something, but Andrej was distracted by some women who came walking up the path. Three beautiful young women, the first of whom was a bleached blonde. Strange that he had never seen them before.

Tudjman said he had always tried to do the right thing, but that a person, after all, was weak at heart. That may well be, Andrej thought, but what's it got to do with me?

"It was me, Andrej," he heard Tudjman say. "I'm the one who blackmailed you all that time."

That was really funny, because as far as he knew, it was the other way around. But maybe he was mistaken; it was like when you totally missed the point of a movie, but you didn't say so and agreed with everyone that it was a good film.

"Why, why?" Andrej asked, and gazed intently as a small group of rabbits hopped down the hill. Suddenly they stopped in a cloud of dust that rose along with a large column of smoke above the lower station, and then they turned and darted back up the hill. He wondered if there was such a thing as a rabbit racetrack.

The three women glanced back, knotted their head scarves under their chins and continued up the hill. Maybe one of them was the woman of his dreams, he thought, and he wanted to wave or call to her, but then he thought: maybe they want nothing to do with me.

"Because I needed money. That's no excuse and I'm sorry, I regret it more than anything I've ever done." Josip began talking faster and faster because he saw the life drain out of Andrej's face. "You didn't deserve it. You're a better man than me. I told Jana all about you and she—"

"Who?"

"My lover. The woman in Zagreb."

The one with the white hat and the nylon stockings, Andrej remembered.

"Yes, I was a good boy," he said dreamily.

Josip removed his cap, took Andrej's right hand, and laid it on his head.

"Can you forgive me?"

"I forgive you," Andrej said, "in the name of the Father, the Son, and the Holy Spirit."

PART 5

They rode to the top of the mountain in a matter of minutes. The century-old carriage was in excellent condition; every wooden seat slat glistened with varnish, the windows were squeaky clean, the brass hardware gleamed. They ascended noiselessly and left the city ever farther behind them.

The carriages carried out their ritual—approach, diverge, pass, and continue—with languid elegance. The conductor was a young woman with blonde curls.

"I know what you're thinking, Josip," Jana laughed and placed a hand on his arm. "Don't look so peevish—these are modern times. Why shouldn't a woman be able to run a cable car?"

"Funicular," he corrected her.

"Yes, of course. Say, aren't you awfully warm? It does suit you, though, that new loden coat. Very German."

Josip unbuttoned the coat and shook his now completely bald head. "Very German? You do know how to rile me!"

"Now, with that white mustache of yours . . ."

"Me, a German!"

"Ach, honeypie, don't act so insulted. You do need a bit of ribbing sometimes. I know you, don't I?"

"Tomorrow," Josip replied. "Tomorrow we'll have been together for fifteen years."

She laid her head on his shoulder. "Yes. It was such a wonderful idea of yours, Josip, this trip."

"Then you really shouldn't tease me."

"You're such a big, strong man—you can take it, can't you?"

"Yes, my darling, but I don't always feel like it. Look, we're nearly there. Are you up for a short walk once we get there, to take in the view?"

"Oh, yes, sure. My hip is like new."

The Neroberg station resembled that of his own funicular, although it was more decorative, with all that filigree woodwork. Their carriage came to a halt smoothly and at exactly the right spot.

They ambled up the path, Jana supporting herself on his arm and her elegant walking stick, and they sat on a park bench near a colonnaded pavilion.

"What a city. I'm so happy we could do all this together, Josip."

Wiesbaden was large, even larger than Zagreb, but most of all it was far prettier. They looked out over the vineyards, the glistening Rhine, and the blue ridge of the Taunus mountains.

"An Orthodox church," Jana said, reading from her guidebook, "with five gilded domes. A duke named Adolf had it built for his deceased wife and child . . . apparently she was a grand duchess from Saint Petersburg. Isn't that romantic?"

Josip remembered that a Russian Orthodox church had once stood on the hilltop above his own funicular, on the spot where they later erected the heroes' monument, of which nothing was left except the base, and which was now used by hang gliders as a takeoff spot.

"It's a few more minutes' walk. Do you want to have a look?"

Josip remained silent and tried to put his hands into his coat pockets, but discovered they were still sewn shut.

The church on his hilltop did not have spires, as far as he could recall. He must have visited it as a child, because he still clearly remembered his first ride on the funicular; it was with his father, and he was madly in love with a girl from kindergarten. He could not remember her name, but she had freckles.

Whether he had gone inside it back then, he did not remember, either.

"No," he decided. "I'll stay here with you."

Jana put the guidebook back into her purse and took out a small stack of postcards.

"Shall we? Look here, I've already stamped and addressed them."

The stamps, commemorating the tenth anniversary of a unified Germany, were emblazoned with little black-yellow-and-red flags.

"To Mario? Why?"

"Why not? He's your oldest friend."

"But not my best one anymore. We haven't spoken in years."

"What of it? I think it's a good idea that he sees we're in Wiesbaden together, even if he's never invited us to that great big house of his with those ostentatious eagles in the driveway. Come on, Josip, just a few words and then our names."

She clicked on the ballpoint pen they had taken from the hotel room. He could not very well refuse. He wrote: *Hello Mario, greetings from sunny Wiesbaden, also from Jana and to your wife and family. Your old friend Josip.*

"There," said Jana. "And now this one."

"To Katarina . . . that's nice of you."

"I do care about her, Josip, you know that. Even though I don't much like going to that asylum with you. Go on, let me send her a greeting."

"You can write it yourself, then," Josip said and handed the card back to her.

Jana pouted, heaved a deep sigh, and started writing. Josip fixed his gaze on the Kurhaus, where the casino was, and thought of Andrej.

"There we are," Jana said. Josip did not read what she had written, but just added *your loving father* at the end.

When they got back to the Neroberg funicular station, the young woman with the blonde curls was filling the ballast reservoir. She was bent over, her feet spread, and wore dark-blue trousers that at least somewhat resembled a uniform, which you couldn't say for her modish psychedelic blouse.

Josip inquired how many passengers were waiting at the bottom.

She answered by holding up a mobile telephone with two large yellow numbers on the display.

Josip looked at the needle on the water meter and said, "Then that'll be enough."

"Really?" she asked and detached the hose. "This is just a vacation job. I don't really know that much about it."

They slept for nearly two hours on the hotel bed, having removed only their coats and shoes. Jana woke up first and switched on the lamp above the headboard.

"Wake up! It's already dark! Time for dinner!"

"Not hungry," Josip mumbled and pressed his face into the pillow.

"You're the one who wanted half pension. We've paid for it, so get up, you!"

But Josip stayed in bed while she turned on all the lights and slid open the sheer curtains in order to look out over the shopping street. He knew she would need at least half an hour before she was ready to go downstairs.

"Look, there's a Zara right across the street! Had you seen it already?"

He did not give a reply, which was not expected from him in any case, and she went into the bathroom. She left the frosted-glass sliding door half-open, for she still believed he found it titillating to watch her perform her ablutions. It was a gesture of intimacy he did not much value anymore.

"What do you think?" she asked, showing him a leg clad in black nylon. "With my new patent leather pumps?"

"Beautiful. Very elegant," Josip said.

She retreated behind the frosted glass without a word. He sat up and rolled his legs out of bed. Where had his shoes gotten to?

Life, on the one hand, had gone by too fast; on the other hand, it dragged on.

What would have happened if he had married the girl with the freckles, whose name he couldn't even remember? And what if there hadn't been a war?

Jana was the love of his life, of course; nothing could ever undo that, and it would be poor form to have regrets now. She was sixty-four, an old woman in fact, certainly after the hip replacement; but he had aged remarkably well, physically at least. Aside from a mild form of diabetes he was completely healthy and he felt as fit as, say, fifteen years ago.

Why, he thought, am I always the one who looks after others—Ljubica, Mirko, Katarina, Jana—and no one has ever looked after me?

The only exception he could think of was during the war, in February 1945.

It was a landscape like none they had ever seen. No one came here, and rightly so: it was barren, inhospitable, well-nigh lifeless terrain. Modrić had a topographical map that promised more variety than what they experienced on a daily basis: there were at least a few numbers, and the curves of the contour lines gave them the sensation they were in another world than one they traversed, which was monotonous and, at the same time, all but impassable. Rain or shine, everything was gray.

The landscape consisted of bare, rocky ridges and deep ravines overgrown with thornbush; in order to follow their compass routes they were constantly fighting their way through the crevices, and after four interminable days of trekking, they were all exhausted.

What a fatherland, Josip thought. Is this what we're fighting for, this wasteland? I hold God responsible.

But they had to press on, because the Germans had captured the entire coastline, and their only chance of survival was to locate the units farther inland. Sixteen men against an enemy army of thousands that was continually reinforced. Fifteen men, actually, because one of them, a reticent cabinetmaker from Split, had shot himself in the head that morning. No one knew why. They lost half an hour looking for loose stones and rocks with which to cover his body, but in the end, the effort being too time consuming, they gave up.

"Leave him there," Modrić had said. "He was a deserter, after all. He betrayed us. That bullet could have been used on a German." And so they left him behind. Josip, despite himself, looked back several times; the buzzards were already circling the spot. They were better informed than the Luftwaffe. Modrić was his commander and therefore he obeyed, but he was troubled by the thought that a person didn't just take his own life for no reason. What could it have been? Maybe something that didn't have to do with the war. The war made you forget that there were other sources of desperation.

But what gave him equal cause for worry was that the sole of his left boot was starting to come loose. If your footwear gave out in a situation like this, you were a goner. The men had the greatest difficulty keeping their balance on the narrow ridges, which offered no foothold to speak of, and which they often had to follow for many kilometers just to cover a few hundred meters as the crow flies. Josip was gripped by panic at the thought that he would not be able to keep up, that he would impede the others, that he would be a liability.

The sole of his boot held out, but his body did not. He realized this when they had to leave the ridge so as not to be spotted by the German reconnaissance planes, and he was unable to clamber back up again. He saw ten meters of thornbushes and ten meters of steep rock face above him and was certain of one thing: he would not make it. His neck suddenly swelled up, as unexpectedly and inexplicably as his member when, as a small boy, he had his first erection. And as frightening, too. He pulled his shirt open to make room for the bulge under his chin that felt like a pelican's overfull throat pouch. He was extremely thirsty but could not swallow. His limbs stopped obeying him.

Mario, who had already reached the top, turned and shouted to him, "Hurry up, Josip! They're gone!"

But he could not. Mario put down his rucksack and rifle and scrambled back down to him. Their commander returned partway and screamed at them.

"Come on," Mario panted, pulling him to his feet.

Josip began coughing hoarsely and collapsed. He soon came to the conclusion that he was no longer a soldier, but a patient. Mario, though, wouldn't accept this.

"Goddammit!" he shouted, close to tears. "Get up, get up!"

He's afraid he'll have to go on alone, without me, Josip thought, and gave it one more try.

There followed a strange, drawn-out procedure; Josip alone in the bushes with nothing more than the blank sky above him, then Mario who returned, Modrić who called him away again, then, as before, nothing but thornbushes and fading shouts, one of which he recognized as Mario's, and finally Mario and four other men who hauled him up the hill.

They carried him over the ridge in a tarpaulin; the path was so narrow that the men had to find their footing lower down, and dragged him along the rock like a sleigh across snowless ground. He was in great pain and lost all control, the cloudless sky offered nothing to focus on; all he saw were the four dark-brown canvas corners of the tarpaulin in which he was cradled, like in a crib, and he was ashamed. They should have left him there, he should have followed the example of the cabinetmaker from Split and done himself in; now his unit was sacrificing manpower and time on his behalf.

Mario knew he could not swallow, and he appeared now and then with his dented canteen and poured lukewarm, valuable water over his face to cool him. Josip saw him as an angel with curly brown hair and large, heavenly eyes who appeared and vanished, but was constantly at his side.

Leave me here, he thought, right now you're only doing the Germans a favor.

But he could not speak, and apparently it had been decided he should be saved.

When he spotted the evening star in the empty sky, they had come upon a place that was more than just rock and thornbush; it was the remains of a barn and a sheep stall consisting of concrete foundation blocks, partially charred beams and slats, and, most importantly, scattered corrugated metal sheets with which his comrades quickly improvised a shelter. Now he lay on sleeping bags embedded in a pit and had a roof over his head for the first time in weeks.

Modrić came to see him and removed his cap to be able to crouch under the corrugated metal roof without banging his head.

"You all right, Tudjman?" he asked.

Josip could not speak, but opened his eyes wide and gestured vehemently with two fingers, as though repeating the horizontal half of the sign of the cross, that no, he was not all right, and they should leave him behind.

"Forget it, Tudjman. You just get better and fight. You won't shake us so easily."

Modrić was not a kind man, and Josip understood all too well that he would have left him behind had it not been for Mario.

"Do you know what this is?" he asked, holding up a small, well-thumbed book. "*Das Feldlazarett*, the field hospital. We found it in the wreckage of that German ambulance we shot up above Gospić, you remember?"

Josip's hand rested on the clammy sleeping bag. He felt like a man who had been given a life sentence and was now waiting to see if he would be given another three life sentences on top of it.

"I'm no doctor. I am—or was—an engineer, as you might know. But your symptoms tell me you've got diphtheria. And this," he said, showing him a small cardboard box, "are injection syringes with penicillin. A miracle drug from America."

It probably lasted no more than two weeks, but afterward it felt like he had spent seasons, years even, under that low corrugated roof where the sun beat down in the morning, and from which gushed parallel streams of water when it rained; a long, long time during which he did nothing but lay there and suffer while his comrades tended to his every need.

Mario was ubiquitous, maintaining a caregiver's aloofness to spare his friend needless shame. Josip was grateful to him.

Even more so because Mario also kept telling him dirty stories, assuming that Josip was still a man, or would be one again soon, instead of a stinking wreck with bloody eyes.

"That Ljubica and her sister, you know, we've got to get our hands on them. They're the sexiest broads in town. Unless we take Berlin and I can get Eva Braun, I'll marry her, and you her sister. What do you think?"

"Fine, it's a deal," Josip said as Mario jabbed the syringe into his thigh. "You get Ljubica and I'll take her sister."

He had a fever and recalled his first infatuation. That was long before those first, worrying erections, because he knew for sure he was still in kindergarten. It was the first time he had gone up on the funicular. She was with her parents, Austrians who were in the diplomatic corps. They were only there for that one summer, his mother had told him, and that's why the girl with the freckles went to the same kindergarten as he did, even though she spoke only German. This made her, in his eyes, all the more desirable. A girl who lived so far away must be something very special indeed, he fantasized. He was convinced that she was the love of his life and thought up a plan to win her over.

He was lucky, because on a seat in the cable car he found an advertising brochure for gleaming white steamships and palm-lined beaches. He stuck it under his shirt while no one was looking.

And when their parents went into the dark church, which the children had no desire to do, he took her behind a small wall with the promise of showing her something very beautiful.

"What, then? What?" she asked, beaming.

She let out admiring squeals at the very first photos, and Josip mustered up the courage to turn the pages one at a time. He would ask her to marry him when he reached the color photo where cheering natives in dugouts surrounded a ship with red smokestacks.

Why that never went through, he couldn't say.

Whenever German reconnaissance planes approached, his comrades took cover underneath the corrugated shelter with him, at close quarters, and he regarded those moments as the happiest in his life. He was afraid and he was grateful and he could hardly believe that they were there with him and had not left him behind.

After that time in the mountains, when he had recovered, it felt as though his life had become infinitely more worthwhile than before, because his comrades had sacrificed so much to rescue him; he felt obliged to repay them in some way and volunteered for the most dangerous missions. But they would not hear of it, and likewise Modrić always kept him behind at the base camp or in the back lines, as though he had become a sort of company talisman. As the months passed, the effect wore off, both with him and with the others, and before long he considered himself just as unexceptional as before, and simply hoped to survive. And survive he did, thanks to the fact that the hand grenade he had thrown through the embrasure of a German bunker on the last day of the war, and which was promptly thrown back and landed at his feet, did not explode.

He was still sitting on the edge of the bed when Jana came out of the bathroom.

Erika, that was the girl's name.

"What's wrong?" Jana asked.

"I can't find my shoes," he said, somewhat despondently.

"You don't fool me, Josip," she said. "I know you. You're just a bit down in the dumps again, that's all. Have you been thinking about her?"

At moments like these, Jana always assumed he was thinking about his late wife.

"Yes," he replied sadly. It might be a barefaced lie, but it was still the easiest way out.

Erika with the freckles returned to Vienna with her parents shortly thereafter, and he never saw her again.

Jana stroked his bald head and said, "Ach, darling, don't. It really is better this way. She simply couldn't cope with life. And I'll be with you always."

"Nur einen Kaffee für mich, bitte," he said after dinner.

"Oh, Josip, only a coffee? Are you sure? No after-dinner slivovitz?"

"Yes, I'm sure," he said gruffly. "I know what I do and don't want."

Extras like that won't be included in the half pension, he thought to himself. She lowered her eyes bashfully and he noticed, not without a certain satisfaction, the surprised and respectful expression on the face of the young waitress when he handed the menu back to her.

Jana reached over to him, and he felt obliged to let her hold his hand.

Her eyes had never really done much for him; in all those years it was more about her expression as a whole, and about her body, of course, her scent, and her stylishness. They were reassuring eyes, to be sure, attractive but not threatening, unlike Ljubica's, which had always been the eyes of an enemy. Jana's look was receptive, searching, expectant, and even her theatrical makeup could not change that. But now she gave him a penetrating look and squeezed his hand, as though to lend weight to the words she was about to utter. He hoped she wouldn't get too emotional. He would listen, of course he had to listen, but he did not expect to hear anything that would add to his happiness; they had been lovers for too long for that. She was his ally, she had earned her place, but he had to be on his guard.

"Josip," she whispered.

Suddenly something uncontrollable welled up in him. I am grateful to her, he realized, my God, I'm grateful. What would have become of me without her? All of a sudden he realized that she, in her own way, had cared for him, too, so lovingly that it more than compensated for all the trouble he had taken, the debts he had settled, to keep her in the style she so desired. This was not the moment for pettiness. There was never a moment for pettiness.

"I thank you, Jana, my darling," he said, pressing his thumbs into the fleshy part of her palm. "I thank you for everything. I should have said this a long time ago . . . I thank you with all my heart for the love you've given me."

"But, Josip . . . ," Jana said with a confused smile, ". . . I was just about to say . . . that I love you so terribly much. You are the man of my life. The only one. I wanted to say . . . that I respect you more than you might ever know. And nothing will ever, ever change that."

"And to think it all started with a personal ad," Josip said, realizing he had gone dangerously far.

"Yes. That's how things go sometimes. And here we are, having dinner together, abroad."

He took her right hand and brought it to his lips, a gallant way of damping down the situation.

"We're together, and we'll stay together," he said when the coffee arrived, to round off the emotionally charged exchange. And he meant it. He was not planning to marry her, because the money in his savings account was intended entirely for Katarina, but he resolved to acknowledge her as his life partner one way or another, for after all those years—and him now a widower—it would not do to regard her as his mistress any longer. He needed time to consider the right approach.

Jana beamed; she looked intensely happy and moved. But there was something afoot. With Jana there was always something afoot, when everything was perfectly in order. That was her specialty.

"You know what I feel like?"

Wiesbaden's casino was renowned. It was there that Dostoevsky, the great Russian author and roulette addict, came to ruin; Josip knew he wrote a memorable novel about it, which he had not read but which still confirmed his opinion that lotteries and games of chance were a scourge on humanity.

For how could money wheedled from the poor and desperate ever lead to anything good, seeing that it would then be paid out—and at most only in part—to just one of them, to the detriment of all the others? He saw it as submitting to fate. If people can survive by the labor of their own hands, he thought, we don't need this—just as we have no use for kings or queens. He was amazed that Tito had not abolished the state lottery.

And Josip had seen firsthand what a gambling addiction could do to a person: the anonymous man who had blackmailed him for years had used it to finance his visits to the casino.

Years later he told Jana about the photographs, threatening letters, and payments and was rather surprised that she thought it an exciting saga. She even asked to see the photos the blackmailer had taken of them at their hilltop rendezvous, but he had burned them long ago.

"You know," she said, "I believe I saw that man back then."

"What?" he asked incredulously. "What did he look like?"

"Oh, I don't know anymore . . . I was otherwise occupied, wasn't I . . . But I remember him being quite tall."

"And what else?"

"He wore a straw hat."

"A straw hat. And why didn't you say anything?"

"Ach," Jana laughed, "I figured it was just a voyeur. It rather excited me, actually."

Not that he held a grudge after all these years. The scoundrel had disappeared from his life for good. Josip no longer hated him. People just did things to one another, and no one was immune to temptation. Andrej was young and therefore died more or less innocent; but even he had bet on the dog races and had sought a shortcut to prosperity by pilfering money from mail he had been entrusted with. Hardly more than a youthful indiscretion, all things considered, while he, Josip, was far more culpable for having blackmailed him about it for so long.

He had done wrong, but not out of malice. That was no excuse, of course—he had succumbed to wrongdoing when the opportunity presented itself.

And when the funicular was under attack, Andrej had sacrificed his life to save the lives of others, including his wife and child, while he himself had done nothing except survive the war, thanks to Mario and his other comrades.

Perhaps it was time to mellow. He was no better than anyone else. Maybe he should go along with Jana's wishes, and not be so high minded.

It was only human, he thought, to give in once in a while. Perhaps even corruption and nepotism had their good side: they at least gave the unfairness of existence a somewhat more human face. It was actually nice of Napoleon to have made those two good-for-nothing brothers kings. The Germans were not corrupt, and look what misery they had brought the world.

Why shouldn't he take Jana to the casino, if she had her heart set on it?

Being able to let go of a principle might mean he was simply evolving as a human being.

He decided to buy one hundred euros in chips. That was, he reckoned, about as much as a fifty-pound note would be worth now. Once they were used up, that would be the end of it.

The Kurhaus was a white temple with classical columns, almost too imposing to just walk inside.

Jana gawked in wonder and nearly choked from the excitement. This could well be the highlight of her life, Josip thought, while he himself tried not to be too impressed by it all. The gaming hall was immense, with dark paneling and enormous chandeliers, and there were six or eight or ten roulette tables, illuminated like green tropical islands. He let her choose where they would play and was not surprised when she chose the table with the best-looking croupier.

"What now?" she whispered. "I want to win."

Josip placed a small chip worth five euros on black; the ball bounced and clattered, and when the wheel slowed down, they saw that it had landed on the number 17, a black pocket. The croupier slid his chip back to him, plus one of the same.

"You see? A win. That's how it works."

Jana whispered, "I've read that the sum of all the numbers on a roulette table is 666—the number of the Beast. Don't you find that macabre?"

"Not at all," Josip replied. He slipped a small stack of chips onto black and lost.

"You shouldn't have done that," Jana said, "because it had just landed on black the time before."

"Gambler's fallacy, my dear. That's not how it works. Chance does not have a memory."

"Well, we'll see about that. I'm a woman, I know more about these things than you do."

Josip thought she was overestimating herself but held his tongue.

"Say, young man," she addressed the croupier, "this is my first time. What would you advise?"

"It is a game of chance, madame," he replied courteously, "and there are many possibilities. There's the 'double street' or the 'column bet' . . . have you read our brochure?"

"Double street," Jana said confidently. "To start, I'll bet everything on double street."

"That means your payout will be eleven to one if you win," the croupier said. *"Faites vos jeux."*

The ball bounced for a long time and when it came to rest, the wheel was still spinning too fast to see whether she had won or lost; they only knew when the handsome young man raked all her chips toward him. Jana was shocked. This was not how she envisioned the evening. Their fellow players—an elderly German couple, a nervous young Asian woman, three drunk English tourists, and a very young man with large blue eyes and a wispy beard—appeared to take no notice at all of the tragedy.

Josip placed another bet, won, and got back twice his stake: he now had twenty euros instead of the five he had started out with.

"Oh, so that's how it's done," Jana said, draping an arm over his shoulders. "Ah, if I only had another little stack of chips . . . *then* you'd see something!"

But Josip shook his head. She'd had her chance, and he was not going to let the visit to the casino cost him more than one hundred euros.

"Then you play for the both of us, darling," Jana said, being a good sport about it. "Go on. I'll bring you good luck, you'll see!"

Josip lost his twenty euros, but still had plenty of chips left.

He worked up a two-hundred-euro profit in a nearly perfect winning streak. He was deep in concentration. It was all perfect nonsense, but if you did something, you might as well do it right.

"Give me a chip, just a small one," Jana whispered, "and you'll see me win."

He relented, and she bet on a single number, the number 15—undoubtedly because tomorrow would mark their fifteen years together—and lost.

"Oh dear," she said, "the odds were thirty-five to one, wouldn't that have been something! Well, at least I have you."

Josip played, won a few and lost a few, but in the end, he won so much that the little towers of chips started to attract the attention of his fellow players.

"Haben Sie ein System?" asked the young man with the large blue eyes.

"Nein," Josip replied. "No system."

And again he won three hundred euros, with a square bet.

Lady Luck was so clearly on his side that he started to become suspicious.

Say he won even more money—a *lot* of money: then it would change his life and that of Katarina, without it really having anything to do with him. This was not good, something like this could not be good. On the other hand, since he had decided to let go just this once, why not enjoy it if he won?

The English tourists got up to try their luck at the slot machines.

Josip hesitated. If he were to get up and go now, he could cash in more than three thousand euros in chips. That was a goodly sum and would give him something pleasant to remember Wiesbaden by. But he had the feeling he was not done yet. It would be more logical to lose it all. He skipped two turns and watched the turning wheel and the skipping ball.

The Asian girl stood up and thanked the croupier with a courteous nod and a chip.

"Merci pour les employés," he said, without budging.

Josip brusquely slid all his chips forward, bet on manque, an easy bet with two-to-one odds, and doubled his capital.

Almost fatalistically, he left it all where it was, and won again. About nine thousand euros now.

It made his head spin; this was not going well, because it was not normal. He took his handkerchief and wiped his forehead.

"A glass of mineral water, please," Jana called out; she squeezed his arm firmly and whispered, "Keep going, keep going! You're on a lucky streak."

He glanced at the elderly couple. They had wagered cautiously, with small bets, but now the man shook his head irritably and put his last chip on a single number: 17.

The young croupier had most likely seen everything by now and did not flinch when Josip placed everything he had on that same number. The chance of it being a winner was less than three percent.

"Rien ne va plus," the croupier said and spun the wheel. The ball bounced, more often, it seemed, on red than on black. The 17 was black.

The wheel slowed, but the ball continued to roll noncommittally over the edges of the pockets, like mercury that refused to settle, but eventually it came to rest.

"Oh, Karli—we've won!" the old woman whispered.

Three hundred and fifty thousand euros.

A distinguished-looking gentleman with silvery temples, impeccably dressed in a dark suit—probably the manager of the casino—appeared next to the croupier.

"Wünschen der Herr weiterzuspielen—viellicht an einem privaten Tisch? A private table?" he enquired.

Josip looked up. A group of onlookers had gathered around their table: players who had abandoned their efforts at neighboring tables to witness a fortune being made—or lost.

The elderly couple and young man with the large blue eyes remained seated, not because they were planning to continue betting, but more like faithful apostles.

Josip was not displeased to be the center of attention. It was unnatural, insofar as it had never happened to him before, except that one time during the war when he had diphtheria.

"No, we're staying right here," Jana said. "That's right, isn't it, Josip? If you just put aside a hundred thousand as a nest egg, and then . . ."

But Josip would not hear of it. He was going to bet all of it. Not just on a single number now, that was insanity, but an "outside bet": red.

"Faites vos jeux," the croupier called out.

The wheel spun, and it felt to Josip as if he had done nothing his whole life but watch a little ball bounce around in a circle.

"Rien ne va plus!" said the croupier.

It suddenly came to him.

If he won, he would use the money to establish a foundation for mentally handicapped women and girls like Katarina. And the foundation would take the name of a hero who had sacrificed himself while rescuing women and children from the burning city: the name of Andrej Rubinić.

That was how it would be, should he win. Then he would have put all that ill-earned money to good use. He had enough to live off. And even if it wasn't the same exact value of the

English banknote where it all began, he felt it was Andrej's money he had gambled with. This way, something good would come of a bad deed, and he would be absolved of his guilt once and for all.

And the foundation's emblem, he thought, would be a pelican, for Andrej's chest had been pierced while he tried to save lives.

But before the ball came to rest, he started to have his doubts, suddenly recalling that Andrej in fact detested pelicans.

The ball skittered capriciously around the wheel, like a young buck determined to try everything before settling down, or like a fawn gamboling in the meadow; but things would work out, they had to work out. There were red pockets aplenty.

He felt a sudden stabbing pain in his heart, a hot glow filled his chest, and all he saw was a red haze.

During the last, slow revolutions of the wheel, when the ball had already come to rest and could no longer budge from its spot—a child on a merry-go-round, a dauphin being presented to the populace—it all was overshadowed by the realization that he was dying, and he did not recognize the child and would never know who the new king would be.

"Oh my God, call an ambulance!" Jana screamed.

Josip lay hunched over on the table, as though he were taking a nap.

The ball had come to rest on the number 1. Red.

"My husband has had a heart attack! Get him to a hospital, quickly!" Jana cried.

Not long thereafter, a personal ad appeared in the Zagreb evening newspaper *Večernji*.

> Girlish, worldly, extremely solvent, culturally-minded lady, early 60s, seeks a decent, attractive, virile, preferably younger man to share the good things in life with. Marriage an option. Number 55694.

ABOUT THE AUTHOR

Photo © 2015 Bob Bronshoff

Martin Michael Driessen is a Dutch opera and theater director, translator, and writer. He is the author of the novels *Gars*, *Father of God*, *A True Hero*, *Rivers* (which was awarded the prestigious ECI Literature Prize), and *The Pelican*. Writing as Eva Wanjek, he cowrote the novel *Lizzie* with highly acclaimed and prize-nominated poet Liesbeth Lagemaat. In 2018 he published a collection of short stories, *My First Murder*. His work has been translated into English, Italian, German, Spanish, Slovenian, and Hungarian. For more information, visit www.martinmichaeldriessen.com.

ABOUT THE TRANSLATOR

Jonathan Reeder, a native of Upstate New York and longtime resident of Amsterdam, enjoys a dual career as a literary translator and performing musician. Along with his work as a professional bassoonist, he translates opera libretti and essays on classical music, as well as contemporary Dutch fiction and poetry. His translated novels include Conny Braam's *The Cocaine Salesman*, Peter Buwalda's *Bonita Avenue*, Bram Dehouck's comic thriller *Sleepless Summer*, and *Tonio* by Adri van der Heijden. Additionally, he has translated novels, essays, and short stories by Mano Bouzamour, Christine Otten, Maarten Inghels, and Rodaan Al Galidi.